THUNDERBOLT

The Jack Courtney Adventures

Cloudburst
Thunderbolt
Shockwave

WILBUR SMITH

WITH **CHRIS WAKLING**

THUNDERBOLT

Piccadilly
PRESS

First published in Great Britain in 2021 by
PICCADILLY PRESS
4th Floor, Victoria House, Bloomsbury Square, London WC1B 4DA
Owned by Bonnier Books, Sveavägen 56, Stockholm, Sweden
www.piccadillypress.co.uk

A CIP catalogue record for this book is available from the British Library.

ISBN: 978-1-84812-855-2
Also available as an ebook and in audio

4

This book is typeset using Atomik ePublisher
Printed and bound in Great Britain by Clays Ltd, Elcograf S.p.A.

Piccadilly Press is an imprint of Bonnier Books UK
www.bonnierbooks.co.uk

For all our young readers and their families
Wilbur Smith & Chris Wakling

1.

I was concentrating so hard on the *beep-beep-beep* of the metal detector probing the ocean bed beneath me that I didn't notice the shark. The little green light in the middle of the detector's circular head winked in time with the beeping which, underwater, sounded more like *blip-blip-blip*. I floated above it, breathing slowly. The mouthpiece tasted rubbery. Silver bubbles swam lazily above me in gentle bursts. If the detector sniffed out metal – a bottle top, the tag of a broken zip, or an old coin, say – the blips would come closer together and the winking would go mental. Though I'd only turned up rubbish all morning, the idea that Amelia or Xander – both of whom were in the water somewhere nearby, conducting their own searches – or I might actually find what we were looking for was compelling.

Blip-blip-blip.

Sand puffed up around the roving detector's head as I swung it gently from side to side.

Blip-blip-blip-blip-blip.

I'd finned my way to the edge of a patch of sea grass and bobbed there for a moment, watching the green tips of the grass swaying in the current. A few metres beyond this underwater lawn the detector had picked up a metallic scent of some sort. I rooted about in a circle, sending up another billowing cloud of sand.

This machine was set to search a diameter of about fifty centimetres. When the *blip-blipping* became a constant whine, I switched to the smaller wand dangling from a lanyard clipped to my Buoyancy Control Device. It searched with a more focused eye. As it homed in, the clicking sped up. Rather than beeping, this one clicked. It sounded a bit like an insistent dolphin.

My fingers, magnified by the glass of my mask, sifted the sand carefully. Before I even saw it, they had closed around something small with a hole in its middle. I realised that – breaking the first rule of scuba diving – I was holding my breath. Lifting the item to inspect it, I heard the rush of bubbles as I let the breath go: not a wedding ring, as I'd hoped it might be, but the ring-pull off a drinks can.

Rather than chuck litter back into the Indian Ocean, I slid it into my mesh bag and looked up to see where Amelia had got to. And that's when I saw the shark, not thirty metres away, the colour and length of a torpedo, gliding towards me.

The in and out of my breathing was suddenly very loud indeed, the column of bubbles above me thickening to a constant mass. The shark, drifting my way, looked utterly at ease, comically chilled in fact.

Though I'd been diving a lot over the last few days, enough

to get very comfortable underwater again, I suddenly felt as out of place as a football boot in a fridge. The shark slipped closer. With an almost imperceptible flick of its tail it veered to my left. But it didn't get any further away. It was circling me. The unblinking dot of its nearside eye took me in. 'What on earth are you doing down here?' it seemed to say.

Fair question.

What was I doing there? There being ten metres underwater, weighed down with metal-detecting kit, just off the coast of Zanzibar.

Searching for treasure, obviously.

It was all Xander's fault. When he heard Mum was planning a trip to Zanzibar, to help put what happened in the Congo behind us – as if anything ever could – he sent me a link to a company selling underwater metal detectors, telling me I should buy one.

I sent him one word back: 'Why?'

In response he sent me another link, to – of all things – a wedding planner's website. It was full of pictures of beaming brides dressed up like meringues cutting pointlessly elaborate cakes, while men wearing cheesy grins and shiny suits tried to look useful by leaning on the same knife.

None the wiser, I re-sent Xander the same one-word question.

Eventually he picked up the phone to explain. Zanzibar, with its white beaches, turquoise sea, cloudless skies and jaunty palm trees, is one of the most popular high-end honeymoon spots on Earth. Newlyweds pitch up there week in, week out, to celebrate getting hitched. Most of them jump in the sea at some point, wearing nothing but their swimming costumes, sun lotion, and their brand-new wedding rings.

Though the sea there is relatively warm, it's still sea, meaning the water is cold enough to cool you down. Cool anything and it will shrink a bit. A newlywed's finger is no exception. If you've not worn a ring before, and many people – particularly men – haven't before they get married, you're likely to think one that fits correctly is too tight, so you buy one that's a bit loose.

Flap about in the cool sea and your brand-new, highly valuable wedding ring is liable to slip off and sink into the sand, lost forever. Unless you look for it with the right kit. Xander had heard of an American guy who found a bunch of wedding rings just off Waikiki beach in Hawaii. That's also a popular honeymoon spot.

The prospect of spending a fortnight lying by the pool, trying not to think about what Dad had done to Mum and me in the DRC, wasn't that tempting. I'd have gone diving anyway to escape my thoughts. Why not give Xander's hare-brained suggestion a shot while I was at it?

If it worked and I turned up something valuable, I could give the proceeds to Mum. Post-Dad, I knew she needed money more than she was letting on. Conservation is expensive work. Perhaps I could actually help out?

Amelia had jumped at the idea. Knowing how much she likes swimming, and guilty at having dragged her through the Congo disaster, Mum invited her on this trip too.

I was fine with that. She's my oldest friend: we've known

each other since our mothers gave birth to us, fourteen years ago now, in the same maternity ward. The bond between us had grown stronger since our time in the Congo, when Dad turned out to be a fraudulent crook and took off. She's never had a relationship with her own father, and I could feel her sympathy for my loss. I was also fine with my newer friend Xander inviting himself along. Some people you just click with instantly, and he and I had seen eye to eye since the day we met at boarding school a year or so ago. He'd bought his own ticket, plus some ultra-high-end detecting kit. So far the only treasure we'd found – the ring-pull, the zipper, the green coin and something that looked like a bit of boat – was worthless – but, pre-shark, I was still feeling hopeful.

Now, with the shark circling me, I'd settle for getting out of the sea alive.

2.

The shark was big. Even accounting for the magnifying effect of my mask, I reckoned it had to be a good three metres long. It swam around me lazily, its mouth hanging open just enough to show off a fearsome set of tapered teeth. Its back was a dirty brown colour with rust-coloured spots along its flanks and its underbelly was a pale grey. The bulk of the thing! I fought to steady myself. I was already pretty low on air, and I knew that panic-breathing would burn through what was left in my tank in no time.

All animals are good at picking up on panic. Sharks, I imagine, are better at it than most. The last thing I wanted to do was broadcast the total helplessness I felt. So I simply floated there in front of the horrible predator, doing my best to return its blank stare.

As I was mounting this impressive defence strategy, I registered a movement out of the corner of my eye. Something orange was approaching. Amelia wears an orange wetsuit. I knew the thing was her, but the thought didn't make sense.

Or rather the only way I could make it make sense was to conclude that she hadn't seen the shark circling me. Xander, searching the seabed nearby, clearly hadn't. But the thing was directly in Amelia's line of sight. Why was she swimming straight towards it?

I broke from my staring competition with the shark, a warning yell rising. The human voice-box is way less effective underwater. My shouting sounded pretty pathetic and didn't halt Amelia's progress. In desperation I waved my hands about – I was still holding the metal-detecting wand, it turned out – but although this at least prompted her to look my way, when we locked eyes – mine wide, hers smiling – she swam straight past me, cutting across to head the shark off.

I couldn't believe it. My heart was a fist in my throat. She didn't flail or swipe at the shark as she approached, just swam cleanly in front of the monstrous fish as if she had right of way. The shark veered towards Xander to avoid her. He cottoned on and jerked upright, his panic apparent through his mask. For a desperate moment I thought the shark would turn and attack. But with another tail-flick it was suddenly thirty, fifty, a hundred metres away, a grey speck swallowed up by the endless blue.

Amelia is a county swimmer. Despite the scuba gear and metal detector, she did a sort of underwater flip and was immediately heading back our way with long slow fin-strokes. I wanted to shout at her. Why on earth had she taken such a risk? But I'd already demonstrated the pointlessness of yelling underwater, so I gave the signal to surface instead.

Since we weren't that deep and hadn't been down much more than twenty minutes we didn't have to pause long on the way up in order to head off the bends. Even so, the delay cooled my temper. She'd taken a chance – an absurd gamble, in fact, swimming straight at it like that – but I couldn't deny she'd done it to help me.

As soon as we were all safely bobbing on the surface, however, she laughed and said, 'Your faces!' and the anger boiled up within me again.

To buy time, I whistled at Pete in the dive boat. It was anchored in the near distance. We'd drifted along the shore and weren't due up for another few minutes. Attentive as ever, he heard me, pinpointed us and returned my wave.

'*My* face?' I said. 'You're lucky you've still got one!'

'The size of the thing,' said Xander, awed.

'Sand tiger shark,' Amelia said by way of explanation.

The words 'tiger' and 'shark' more than outweighed plain old 'sand' for me. I told Amelia so.

'They're no relation to actual tiger sharks. I wouldn't have told one of them where to go. Sand tigers are harmless. Unless you're a very small fish, or something already dead.'

'How could you be sure?' Xander asked. He knows Amelia pretty well, but not as well as I do. Challenging her knowledge rarely turns out well.

She narrowed her eyes and said, 'Well, a sand tiger is brown on top and yellowy-grey underneath, which I imagine you spotted. It also has a flattened, conical snout and its mouth extends back beyond its eyes, which are small. The big teeth you saw are smooth, not serrated. You'd have to have been a bit braver to notice that, and swum as close to it as I got. Those teeth are for hooking up smaller fish rather than ripping out lumps of whale. But it wouldn't have been hunting, not now. They're nocturnal feeders.'

'You were confident enough about all that to risk annoying it?' Xander muttered.

'Er, yes.'

I tried not to smile.

'Look, it was obviously discombobulating you. I just wanted to –'

'She means it was freaking me out,' I explained to Xander.

The noise of the approaching boat rose over our conversation. It's pretty loud. Pete Saunders, the guy Mum hired to help us out with our underwater treasure hunt, is rightly proud of it. Pete's an ex squaddie – British army – turned dive instructor and he bought the boat new after selling up at home and moving here, to Zanzibar. It's worth ten times the shack he rents. I know because he told me so. The boat, called *Thunderbolt*, is Pete's thing. He has a shaven head and wears huge wraparound sunglasses day and night, and looks a bit like a boiled egg felt-tipped with a superhero mask as a result. He takes his job – getting his clients to dive sites, helping with the equipment, and generally keeping us safe – dead seriously.

'You're up nine minutes early. Everything all right?'

'Sure,' I said.

I could see the thought going through Amelia's head: everything hadn't been all right, because we – or I – had been spooked by a shark, but now we'd surfaced without incident, so nothing bad had happened, so I was technically correct. She kept her mouth shut, and because of that I had to come clean.

'Truth is, we met a pretty big shark down there. It rattled me. But Amelia shooed it away.'

'Basking shark?' Pete asked her.

'Sand tiger,' she explained.

Helping me out of my buoyancy vest, Pete patted me on the shoulder. 'I'm not surprised it shook you up. They look the real deal. But sharks – any of them – very rarely attack. It's the stingrays you want to keep onside. They're more dangerous.'

Xander looked sceptical.

'It's true,' said Pete. 'But even then, the chances of an unprovoked attack are infinitesimal. Anyway, how'd you get on before the interruption?'

I explained our slim pickings.

'Ah well,' he said. 'There's always this afternoon. I've got a good feeling about it.'

'A good feeling?' said Amelia. 'Based on what, exactly?'

I was busy stowing our used tanks, Velcro-strapping them into the rack in the hold. Over my shoulder I said, 'Don't worry, Pete – no need to answer that.'

'I wasn't about to.' He'd only known Amelia a couple of days but had already got the measure of her unique brand of literal genius.

'I can't make you,' said Amelia, her voice deadpan.

Pete's sunglasses glinted darkly against the ocean glare as he busied himself wiping down the boat's controls. Once he'd done that he said, 'Lunch then. Your mum's waiting for us back at base.'

'Good, I'm hungry,' I said.

Pete nudged the throttles forward gently and *Thunderbolt*'s twin Yamaha outboards bit the turquoise water. The back of the boat dipped as the prow rose. Where there had been turquoise stillness all around us, brilliant white-water now boiled in our wake.

I knew – because Pete had proudly told me before I'd been in the boat ten minutes – that each of those outboards was capable of producing 350 horsepower. Between them they could propel us upwards of seventy miles an hour. But Pete was restrained today, barely pushing above idle as we cruised back up the coast towards Ras Nungwi and the swanky resort Mum had decided to treat us to.

I stood beside him at the wheel, one hand gripping the central console. 'Very tranquil,' I said, and sensing he'd need little encouragement, added, 'but don't be shy of letting rip.'

That was a mistake.

Not because Pete wasn't up for it, but because of what happened when he grinned and unleashed a bit of power. As the boat surged across the water its hull, beyond the plane, hit a rhythm, and slapped one-two-three shallow wave-tops reasonably hard. Nothing unusual in that. Except, with the fourth bounce, one of the metal tanks I'd supposedly stowed came loose and bounced clean across the boat's fibreglass deck.

I hadn't tightened the Velcro strapping properly. As bad luck would have it, the base of the heavy canister hit a cleat, hard, snapping it from the gunwale, and leaving a split in the boat's pristine whiteness. I'd heard the thump of the tank hitting the hull above the noise of the engine and wave-slap. So had Pete. Instantly he cut the throttle and, as the speedboat slewed to a standstill, we both turned around to see the offending oxygen tank rolling about in the bilge.

'That looks expensive,' said Amelia. 'Also annoying.'

You'd think I might have resented her for saying that, but damaging Pete's pride and joy had made me feel so immediately sick that the realisation I could pay to have it mended was actually a huge relief.

'I'm so sorry. Completely my fault. I'll pay for the repair, of course.'

I could just make out Pete blinking at me through his sunglasses.

'No,' he said quietly. 'I should have checked the fastenings.'

'I don't think Jack sees it that way,' Xander pointed out.

Pete tried to make light of the mistake. 'Worse things have happened at sea,' he said. But he couldn't stop himself lashing the oxygen tank back in place with a harshness that undercut the joke.

'I'm sorry,' I repeated.

'Easy mistake to make,' he said evenly. 'Try not to let it happen again.'

I'd almost have preferred him to be outwardly angry with me, but he didn't say anything further. After we moored up, I walked the length of the quay slowly. Pete hadn't examined the boat in front of us, but when I turned back from the shelter of the pines fringing the beach, I saw him bent down in the stern, inspecting the damage.

3.

Mum wasn't sunbathing on the white sand beach or kicking back by the pool. She wasn't sipping fizzy water under the striped awning of the bar or making an early start on lunch in the waterfront restaurant either. No, she was in her suite, online, doing some research. She looked up guiltily when I knocked and entered, but the last thing I wanted to do was make her feel bad. If I'd had a tough time in the Congo, she'd been to hell and back.

We were supposed to be here relaxing, blotting out what had happened to us, but neither of us is particularly good at lounging around doing nothing and Mum's idea of a good time is to do some good. Though she'd couched the trip as a holiday, for Mum it was all about protecting the Indian Ocean's coral. We'd already seen bleached skeleton reefs right here off Zanzibar, and Mum was looking into who was responsible for protecting marine habitats in this part of the world. That didn't surprise me. It was her version of our treasure hunt, finding something valuable to do with her time.

'Detect anything?' she asked, snapping the screen shut.

'No, but we will,' I replied. 'Probably.'

Sunlight pouring in across the bureau illuminated the side of Mum's face and neck. Her cheekbone seemed sharp, her jawline too. She's a strong woman but the ordeal in Kinshasa had taken its toll on her. Never mind being held captive all that time, the revelation that her own husband – my father – had staged the entire kidnapping was a bombshell that blew our little family apart.

She wouldn't let him back into the house. I didn't blame her. I wanted nothing more to do with him myself. It struck me, as I put my arm around her bony shoulders, that I hadn't told her I'd reached that conclusion myself, and before I knew what I was doing I was putting the mistake right.

'You do know I'm glad we're shot of Dad, don't you?'

She went very still within my hug.

'Obviously I wish he hadn't done it, but he did. He lied to us both. He had you locked up by thugs, for God's sake. I don't care that he's my father, I'll never forgive him for doing that.'

She took a breath to say something, but held back.

'What is it?'

'I don't know,' she said. 'I really don't.'

'Don't know what?' She was shivering lightly. 'What's the matter?' I asked. 'What are you frightened of?'

She twisted away from me, stood up, folded her arms, fighting to compose herself. 'Nothing,' she said firmly. 'You deserve to know the truth.'

14

'Er, I do know the truth. It was Amelia and I who pieced it together.'

'I don't mean about the kidnapping,' she said slowly. She looked at me steadily. Spokes of brightness bisected her irises. 'I mean about your father.'

'What more is there to know? He's a lying, greedy . . .'

I petered out. The intensity of her gaze was extraordinary. I swear I knew what she was about to say in the nanosecond before she said it: the revelation made complete sense as it landed, clumping into perfect place like an expensive car door.

'Nicholas Courtney isn't your father,' she said.

So simple a sentence, yet to begin with the words refused to make sense. If Dad – Nicholas Courtney – wasn't my father, then that meant I wasn't a Courtney at all. But the family name defined me. It stood for endeavour and guts and not backing down.

He'd tainted it himself of course, but after discovering Dad was a crook, I'd felt more for the family name, not less. It was all the more my responsibility to uphold what it really stood for. And now Mum was telling me that the man who'd given it to me was not my real dad. I was dumbstruck.

'Jack,' Mum whispered. 'Say something, please.'

'I knew it,' I replied, surprising myself. A sudden rush of understanding made everything click into place. That's right, now that she'd spelled it out, the brutal fact of Nicholas Courtney not being my real father made sense of a lifetime of doubt. I had never wanted to admit it to myself, but he – 'Dad' – had always treated me coldly, made me feel somehow unworthy. I thought it had to do with my brother Mark's accident. And perhaps my part in Mark's death did make things worse. But in truth he'd treated me differently when my brother was alive too.

'He was Mark's father though, wasn't he?' I said.

Mum nodded.

'But not mine.'

She shook her head, tears welling in her eyes. 'I'm sorry.'

'Why?' A strange feeling was rushing through me, odd because it was out of place. Of course, sadness and confusion were bubbling up as well, but the main sensation I experienced as the news sank in was relief. 'In a way that makes things easier,' I said under my breath. 'For me, if not you. You chose to be together. Now you've chosen to be apart. But I couldn't be, not until now. Now I'm free. I don't have to think about his blood running through my veins.'

'He's been good to you in many ways,' she whispered. 'But he isn't your father. He always knew it. Now you do too.'

The obvious question came hot on the heels of this admission. If the businessman and crook Nicholas Courtney wasn't my father, who was? Something about the way Mum wasn't volunteering the information made me scared to ask, but I steeled myself to do so regardless.

'Who is?'

'What's that?'

'You know what I mean.'

'Who's who, Jack?'

She obviously didn't want me to ask, but all this pretending she didn't know what I was on about only made me want to know more badly. 'My real father,' I said. 'Who is he?'

Now it was her turn to put an arm around me. I allowed her to pull me close. Her hair smelled of apples. 'It's complicated,' she said.

'That's not an answer.'

'I know,' she said, 'but in a way it is.'

The way she was holding me and her soothing tone reminded me of when I was much younger. She'd held me like that in the days and weeks after Mark died. Then, it felt like she was protecting me from myself. What was she trying to protect me from now? After what we'd just been through, I'd surely proved myself capable of withstanding more or less anything. I shrugged her off gently and said, 'Come on, Mum, I want to know.'

She stood back, stared at me steadily. Did she not want to tell me because she couldn't? As in, did she not know herself? I nearly backtracked. The words 'It doesn't matter' were on the tip of my tongue. But even that – my own mother not knowing who my father was – I could have handled. It would have been an answer of sorts.

She reached out and stroked the side of my cheek with one finger. I couldn't help it; I leaned away. Instantly I felt guilty. I'm glad I didn't cave in though, because she broke the silence eventually, with a promise.

'You have my word: I'll tell you when it's time,' she said. 'Just as I was always planning to do.'

Though I wanted to ask her what 'when it's time' depended upon, I couldn't. It would have felt cruel somehow if I'd pushed further in that moment. Mum moved back to her little hotel desk and tidied it pointlessly. The conversation was over.

She had never lied to me before. I had no reason to doubt she was telling me the truth now: she had a plan and would follow through. And in any case, I knew for a fact that I would never take 'no' for a final answer to this question. It was too important. One way or another, no matter how long it took, I'd work out the answer.

I watched Mum busying herself and saw more clearly how the strain of these last weeks had taken their toll. Beneath the bright Zanzibar sun her skin, which normally tanned so easily, was still pale and papery. And she'd lost weight she couldn't afford to lose. But she'd also lost confidence somehow. She moved with a brittleness I'd not noticed in her before.

'You guys will need to fuel up at the buffet bar,' she said, 'before throwing yourselves back into your underwater hunting.'

'Sure,' I said, and I followed her out into the dappled courtyard, thinking that of all of us she was the one who most needed feeding up.

4.

That afternoon, on Pete's advice, we searched off a different beach. He ran us down to it in the boat. We went gently. He'd already made a temporary repair to the fibreglass damaged by the sheared-off cleat. Noticing the split was neatly covered with gaffer tape, I looked away guiltily. Though this stretch of sand was smaller, one of the most exclusive resorts on the island sat above the beach, meaning wealthy guests. We dropped anchor not far offshore to gear up. A breeze pulled up ridges in the sea. They weren't big waves, but enough to rock the boat beneath my feet.

'Low tide in an hour, so you're best off searching close in,' said Pete.

I steadied myself on the rail near the stern, nodded to Amelia and Xander, then tipped back off it into the sea. The view through my mask was an instant explosion of bubbles.

When they cleared and I surfaced, Pete threw the detectors down to me. Amelia was sorting herself out on the other side of the boat. Xander had also dropped in. I bit down on the regulator, took the first metallic breath of oxygen, and rolled forward to swim beneath the boat and join them.

As I swam well beneath the hull – there was no way I was going to risk scraping it – I met not only Amelia and Xander, but also a large leatherback turtle, a metre across at least, flapping unhurriedly between us. It was swimming at an angle towards the shore. Without so much as a glance at each other we all fell in behind it. The leatherback didn't swim so much as pulse, beckoning us on.

I'm not superstitious, but that turtle struck me as a sign. We kept a respectful distance, swimming side by side behind the leatherback, with the seabed rising to meet us. When the water was no more than ten or twelve feet deep, and we were not far from the beach at all, the turtle veered away, and again, without communicating to each other, we all stopped. Quite clearly this was the spot to start our search.

This wasn't the shallowest place we'd scoured. The previous afternoon I'd run the detector so close to shore I could have stood up, but the aqualung was still a huge help: with just a snorkel I'd have been duck diving and resurfacing every thirty seconds.

Now, even though the serrated surface of the sea was almost within reach, I could hang a couple of feet off the seabed and search systematically. The blip-blip-blip of the detector was a familiar and soothing soundtrack. I worked my way methodically along the beachfront. Any moment now, I said to myself.

Any. Moment. Now.

For a good twenty minutes, all I heard was blip-blip-blip.

Life is disappointing, I thought.

Dad, I felt.

The detector rummaged a dead starfish from the sand.

There was snot in my mask. I bit the mouthpiece hard.

Sea is salty.

So are tears.

Where the hell were Amelia and Xander, anyway? The drill was to stick close together but occasionally one of us strayed. I swivelled to look for them and immediately the metal detector's flash-blipping shot up in tempo.

Sculling backwards kept me – and it – in place.

The blipping became a constant hum.

I pulled out the focused probe and zeroed in on what I'd found, knowing it would be a hair clip or the arm off a pair of sunglasses or maybe a bit of tin can, but hoping for something better all the same. The dolphin-clicking of the probe quickened to a white line of noise. I dug my fingers beneath its tip and gently sifted the sand. Something glittered in the refracted sunlight. A ring. White gold or platinum, heavy either which way, a thick hoop of wedding ring. Up close, magnified by my mask, I could make out engraved markings on the ring's inner edge.

Amelia had seen me stop. I looked up to find her at my side. Xander also cottoned on and joined us. Amelia held out a hand. I placed the ring on her palm. She inspected the ring and gave me a thumbs-up. In diving a thumb jerked upwards is a signal to your diving partner to surface, but I knew what she really meant and replied with the correct hand sign, my thumb and forefinger held in an 'OK' circle.

She returned the ring to me and I put it in the net bag clipped to my BCD. I was concentrating as I did this, double-checking the thing was secure, but something made me pause. The detectors were out of synch; one of them was blipping faster than the other. They were probably just set that way, I thought, fastening the bag shut. But no, one set of blips was definitely speeding up. I looked down and saw that Amelia's detector, dangling behind her on its lanyard, was the culprit.

She hadn't noticed, but quickly turned around when I pointed. With me having just found exactly what we were looking for right here, her machine had to be on a hiding to nothing. But she worked the sand with it, zeroed in on whatever had set the detector off, and used her probe as I had done to locate whatever metal thing was buried in the sand. When she dug the thing out and held it up I just about spat out my regulator.

She'd found another ring.

'Incredible!' I shouted, though of course it just came out as garbled bubbles.

Amelia blinked at me, her eyes massive in her mask-squished face.

Xander gave the signal to surface and up we went. Since we hadn't been deep, we didn't have to hang around to decompress. We simply popped up into the brightness.

'That's unbelievable!' Xander said once he'd spat out his regulator.

Amelia, still clutching the ring in her fist, pushed her mask up onto her forehead with her other hand and said, 'Why?'

'Eh? Nothing for days then two rings not ten feet apart!'

'It makes adequate sense to me,' she said.

'Sense?' I chipped in. 'Monumental luck, more like.'

'No, it makes obvious sense. Think about it.'

She was serious. When that happens it's best to be serious back; she's usually a step ahead. Side by side, afloat on the glassy swell, we floated while she waited for us to catch up.

'Go on,' I said. 'Help me out.'

5.

'We're looking for rings that have fallen off newlyweds' fingers,' said Amelia.

'Yeah.'

'And I agree that finding two such rings in the same ten-foot by ten-foot patch of sand would be improbable.'

'Impossible, more like.'

She did that eye-narrowing thing she does when she's about to point out something illogical, but today she decided to let my 'impossible' slide. Instead she said, 'So if two accidents in the same place would be improbable, and yet there were, incontrovertibly, two rings in the same patch of sand, we have to assume it wasn't an accident, meaning somebody dropped or threw the rings in the sea on purpose.'

'Who the hell would throw away valuable jewellery?' asked Xander.

'I agree, it's a stupid thing to do. But these are wedding rings. Hitching yourself to another person for life isn't that bright in the first place, in my opinion. What if that person changes? Everyone does. And when it happens, if you don't like the change, and the marriage goes sour, well, people do all sorts of weird things.'

'Like lob their rings into the Indian Ocean.'

'Exactly.'

'But this is a honeymoon resort!'

'Not exclusively. And anyway, some marriages are so stupid they collapse immediately.'

Pete had arrived in the boat. Its outboards idled gently. With my ears above water, the noise was a throaty gurgle, but when I leaned my head back into a wave the sound was more a buzz.

'Told you so,' said Pete before we'd even explained what we found. 'Didn't I? I said I had a lucky feeling about this afternoon.'

I let Xander reveal the full extent of that luck as we climbed aboard. Pete raised his wraparound sunglasses, whistled, and said, 'You're kidding me.'

'What would be the point of such a deception?' said Amelia.

'I still don't get why they'd throw away valuable jewellery,' Xander muttered, inspecting our find. 'These rings are heavy. They must be worth a bomb. Why not just sell them?'

'That's unknowable,' Amelia replied. 'Though symbolic acts are a thing.'

I was stowing my kit, double-checking the straps very carefully indeed. Amelia was looking the rings over closely. 'The hallmarks match, meaning they were made by the same jeweller, which supports my theory.'

'How much do you think they're worth?' I asked.

'Together, a few thousand pounds,' said Amelia. 'Maybe even as much as ten! Great, eh?'

I had a plan for my share. Raising awareness of the plight of the coral reefs costs money. I wanted to contribute to Mum's work, but since the only cash I'd ever had came from her I'd just be giving her back her own resources. Now I could actually add to her much depleted – thanks, 'Dad' – war chest. I'd not yet told Mum this was what I intended to do. The idea was I'd hand over whatever I found at the end of the trip. And now I had something to give. A warm glow spread through me as I thought how happy she'd be when she realised that's what all the detecting had been about.

'It's a good start,' I said.

'Because it's a good plan.' Xander shrugged modestly.

'Self-evidently,' said Amelia.

Turning to Pete I said, 'Any idea when you might have that lucky feeling again?'

6.

We returned to Ras Nungwi and helped Pete sort out the boat before stepping ashore. Even after we'd tied up to the jetty and put everything down in the hold for the night, he fussed about wiping down the controls, seats and surfaces with a big chamois leather. This just made me feel worse about my carelessness earlier. He sensed as much: as we walked up the gangplank he put a hand on my shoulder and said, 'Don't worry about it, Jack. A split boat seam can be mended. Think about what went right today.'

I saw my face reflected in his dark glasses, blinking, and the thought went through my head: if I'd trashed something of 'Dad's' he wouldn't have let me forget about it for weeks.

It was Pete who blurted out our success to Mum, as soon as we found her. 'Not one but two rings, on the same dive. Platinum or white gold. Didn't I tell you I'd take them to good spots?'

There had been more at stake in our search for him than I realised, I saw.

'Bright and early tomorrow?' asked Pete.

'Stay for dinner. Celebrate,' said Mum.

Pete mumbled something about errands he had to run.

'We won't actually be eating for an hour and a half,' Amelia pointed out. 'Plenty of time to do all that and come back.'

Once we'd persuaded him to return later, I headed to my room for a shower, and when I got back to the beachfront bit of the hotel Amelia, who'd beaten me to it, was talking with Mum and Xander about Mum's coral reef destruction research. I arrived to hear Amelia say, 'Oh yeah, fan coral. It looks a bit like marbled ham. Decimated by sixty per cent?'

'You'd be interested in what I dug up online,' said Mum. 'I'll get my laptop.'

I hadn't yet sat down, so I offered to fetch it for her. She thanked me and handed me the key to her room. I ambled off through the palm trees, sand dusting the boardwalks, scratchy beneath my bare feet.

On my way I passed a young girl, no more than eight years old, carrying a pile of freshly laundered towels. She stuck in my mind as, when I entered Mum's room, I came upon another girl who, though not as small as the first, was definitely younger than me.

She'd turned Mum's bed down and was placing a wrapped chocolate on the pointlessly large pile of pillows. I waited awkwardly for her to leave. That she was younger than me somehow made the situation worse. She did a lot of smiling and nodding and saying nothing as she backed out of the door.

Mum's laptop was on her dressing-table/desk. When I disconnected the mouse the screen came to life. I would never have intentionally invaded her privacy by looking at what was on it, but something on the screen caught my eye before I could look away. It was a new message box. The image was small, floating at the top left of the screen in front of whatever Mum had been reading, a headshot accompanied by some text.

The words read: *Hard to say exactly. It's only a short flight, I know, but I've a proper mess to sort out here first. Believe me, I'm doing my damnedest. This meeting is as important to me as it is to you and him.*

Out of context this message didn't mean much, and I like to think I wouldn't have read it all if I hadn't first noticed the face of the man I assume sent it, hovering next to the text. The headshot was all of a centimetre wide, so the man's eyes were little more than pinpricks, but something about the set of them – wide-spaced in his face, watchful under a determined brow – together with his square chin, drew me up short. I couldn't work out why to begin with. I recognised him somehow. I'm good with faces: I tend not to forget them. But I'd never met this guy, as far as I could remember. And yet I knew him. His face, or a version of it, swam in every reflective surface I'd ever seen.

This meeting is as important to me as it is to you and him.

I shut the laptop and carried it in a daze back to Mum. She didn't blink at the message, just clicked it shut and got on with showing Amelia the coral reef research papers she'd dredged up. I'd already tuned out. I was thinking about

29

Mum's earlier promise, when I asked her to tell me who my real father was. 'I'll tell you when it's time,' she'd said. When would that be?

For some reason I couldn't get the words *hard to say exactly* out of my head. *I've a proper mess to sort out here first* also reverberated, and so did *it's only a short flight*. Mum had suggested this Zanzibar holiday to help us get away from everything, or at least that's what she'd said.

Had she in fact been bringing us closer to the man who sent that message? To ask her I'd have to let on that I'd read it. Though I hadn't meant to intrude, I didn't want to admit I had and risk losing her trust in me.

'You're a lot of fun this evening,' said Xander, turning to me. He'd also obviously lost interest in Mum and Amelia's coral-cataloguing conversation.

'Sorry, yeah. Miles away.'

'I could see that. What are you thinking about so hard?'

'Kids,' I said. I hadn't planned to. I just blurted it out.

'Eh?'

'They employ kids in this hotel, doing the laundry, cleaning the rooms. I just saw two girls who work here, both younger than me.'

Xander nodded. 'There was a boy scrabbling about in the flowerbed out front when my cab pulled up. I thought he must have lost something. But he was digging weeds. He was tiny. Eight or nine at most.'

Amelia took a breath. I've heard her do so a million times. Generally, it's a sign she's going to set me straight on something. Now was no exception.

'You realise kids our age have it rougher than us all over the place. We're the exception, not the rule?'

'Sure, but –'

'The chambermaids and gardeners they employ here should still be in school, but many kids are even worse off. Those boys and girls we saw digging with their bare hands in the Congolese mines, for example. Remember how hopelessly exploited they were? Well, even they are lucky compared to some.'

'How?' asked Xander.

'Most of the world's nastiest conflicts involve child soldiers one way or another. Theirs has to be the bleakest existence. All sorts of evil gangs and militia and even state armies force kids our age and younger to run chores for soldiers, man checkpoints themselves, act as spies and in the worst cases fight on the front lines. It's a fact: kids are pretty much used as cannon fodder, all over the place. For example, in Somalia, just up the mainland coast, there are children fighting for the government and every other warring faction, including the dreaded Al-Shabaab. They're Islamic terrorists,' she said, second-guessing my blank look. 'Jihadist fundamentalists, linked to Al-Qaeda.'

I looked out across the terrace, twinkling with fairy lights now, while Amelia expanded on the dreadful conflict in Somalia. She talked of the country's problem with pirates, so desperate that they'd risk attacking international boats protected by armed guards.

Beyond the terrace lay the shifting surface of the sea, studded with reflected stars. It was a beautiful sight. So tranquil, in fact, that it made it hard to believe what Amelia was saying, though I knew she was telling the truth.

Lounging around in this luxurious resort, eating great food, with only the excitement of diving for treasure to worry about . . . we had it good, I knew that. But weirdly, although I felt sympathy for all those kids working for a pittance or being forced to fight in wars, I also resented having to think about them at all. Their problems weren't my fault and I couldn't do anything to help them, could I?

Luckily Pete arrived at that moment, distracting me. He was dressed in a Hawaiian shirt, which immediately brought my uncle Langdon to mind. Pushing that unwelcome thought aside I said to Xander, 'Actually, I was thinking about where we might dive tomorrow. What's the plan, Pete?'

The dive instructor immediately launched in with suggestions. Xander had done his research. He seemed to know the spots as Pete brought them up. Either that, or he was doing his excellent-with-adults thing again.

I could tell he wanted to be as excited by our find as I was, and his enthusiasm spurred mine on: by the end of the evening I'd pushed aside the message I'd seen on Mum's computer. I couldn't do anything about it anyway. I went to bed so keen to get up and dive again in the morning that I found it hard to sleep.

7.

We worked our way around the island's pristine coastline over the following days, expertly guided by Pete. He dropped us in all the best spots, close to the island's honeymoon epicentres, and he tended the boat while we searched the seabed, kept a watch on what was happening above the water, warning away the odd speedboat and jet-ski that strayed too close, making sure nothing ran us down when we surfaced.

We searched and searched with our detectors. The three of us egged each other on to do more dives and stay out longer, meaning we spent the maximum possible time we could hunting for treasure in those turquoise shallows.

Why the intensity? Because we were successful again, and success was like a drug: the more we had, the more we wanted.

We never repeated the two-rings-in-one-dive result, and we turned up a hell of a lot of rubbish, from tiny fish hooks so small that only Xander's detector spotted them, to a complete anchor and chain which somebody must have slung overboard without checking it was attached to the boat. The only way we could retrieve this hulking mess was to swim down to it with a bit of rope, tie that to the chain-end, and swim clear to let Pete winch it up into the launch.

He wasn't best pleased to see the rusty thing bleeding out in his immaculate white hold. But he was as delighted as we were when we turned up a slim ring the following morning, and we were yet more excited about the one after that, a fatter ring studded with tiny diamonds flush to its platinum surface.

In all, over the next seven days, we found five valuable rings. Xander and Amelia found two each, and I found the last one, a single band of gold. Xander also pinpointed a gold earring that morning. Together with the engraved pair of wedding rings Amelia and I started with, that meant we'd sniffed out eight pieces of actual treasure in a little over a week and a half.

And we still had a bit of time left. But with the end of the trip in sight, I began to feel antsy, and not just because it meant an end to our metal detecting. If my hunch was right, and Mum had chosen Zanzibar because of what – or who – was nearby, we were running out of time to make use of that fact.

Mum seemed completely unconcerned: all she was worried about was how to further her coral conservation work beyond Zanzibar. Doubts crept in about the message I'd seen. How could I be sure of anything from a thumbnail-sized photograph? And the wording had been ambiguous: it could have meant more or less anything. Despite this, when I found myself alone at the breakfast table with Mum on our penultimate morning, I couldn't quite hold my tongue. She was picking at a fruit salad; I had a plate of waffles swimming in maple syrup and cream. Amelia was churning laps in the hotel pool as she did every morning, even though we were going to spend much of the day underwater. 'It's exactly the opposite type of swimming,' apparently. Xander hadn't yet got up. I took a sip of iced coffee and felt the question simmering inside me. I didn't want to ask it again, as I say, but as I stirred the ice cubes in their vortex of froth, it came out.

'When are you going to tell me who he is?'

This time Mum didn't pretend not to know what I was talking about. 'When the time's right, I promise,' she said with a regretful smile.

'That's pretty vague.' I fought to keep the frustration from my voice. 'You have to admit.'

'I'm sorry, Jack,' she replied, without offering anything further.

'Me as well.'

She spoke slowly, picking her words carefully. 'It's a sensitive situation. But trust me, I'm working on it.'

I had a strong urge to throw the remains of my coffee at the bamboo wall beside me. The ice would have clattered off it satisfyingly. But I didn't. I took another bite of waffle instead, then pushed the plate aside: though hard to believe, there's such a thing as too much syrup.

Xander arrived, having just stepped out of the shower

by the look of him. His hair was scraped back from his forehead in wet black furrows. He and Mum immediately struck up a conversation about dolphins. We'd seen some the previous day. Xander had been closest, right in among the pod as they swam past us. Mum wanted to hear all about it again and Xander, true to form, entertained her politely, when I'm sure he'd have preferred to talk gibberish with me.

Amelia, who'd finished her laps in the pool, sat down with a huge bowl of banana-topped porridge. She tucked into it unhurriedly. The knot of tension tightened in my chest. Those ice cubes really needed chucking hard at something. What was with everyone? Why the lack of urgency?

'I'm going to get ready,' I said. 'We don't have much more time and I want to push our total finds above ten.'

'What's so special about the number ten?' asked Amelia.

'Nothing!' I said. 'It's just a target. Better to have one than not.'

'Sure,' said Xander sceptically. He was eyeing Amelia's breakfast. 'Can I just eat something first?'

'Whatever. I'll be down at the jetty helping Pete.'

He looked at me quizzically then, and that was fair enough: he'd done nothing to annoy me so why was I being so short with him? Just . . . because. I didn't need to explain myself. I stood up, said, 'See you later,' without looking at either of them, and walked off.

8.

The previous day Pete had mentioned an island set apart from the Zanzibar archipelago, with an exclusive resort where the truly fabulously wealthy stayed. I'd immediately wanted to search there.

But with his next breath Pete had said he thought there would be slim pickings off the little beach. 'Exclusive' meant small. The place only hosted a handful of guests at any one time, making it less likely that there'd be many lost valuables to detect on the seabed. Though disappointed, I had let the subject drop.

Approaching the marina now, I changed my mind. So what if only a few guests stayed at the place? Over the years that would still amount to a fair number of people. And they'd be properly loaded, dripping with bling probably.

How much did billionaires spend on jewellery? More than anyone else! We would only have to find one ring to make the trip worth our while.

Pete was polishing the boat's fuel gauge when I arrived.

...d him I wanted to dive off the island he'd mentioned, where the poshest of the posh stayed.

'As I said, I think that's a real long shot, searching there.'

'I don't care. The longest odds often mean the biggest winnings.'

'It's a good hour away by boat. Even this one,' he said.

'So?'

He raised his sunglasses onto the polished dome of his head and looked at me askance. 'You OK?'

'Of course.' I tried to soften my tone. 'I just meant it'll be a fun ride. The weather's good. Why don't we give it a go?'

'You haven't got a great deal of time to play with.'

'I know. But like your good feeling the other day, I've got a hunch this will pay off.'

He was polishing the twin throttle levers now, though their chrome stalks were already gleaming.

'It's your call,' he said.

I took that as a yes, and to show I was grateful I made myself useful preparing the boat for the day. It needed more fuel. Pete had magicked up a couple of big plastic jerry cans from somewhere. When I lifted one from the hold to pour it in, the thing weighed a ton. Warily, I asked for a funnel.

Correctly guessing that I was worried about slopping petrol all over his precious boat, Pete laughed and said, 'Don't bother with that. Use a siphon instead,' and he showed me how to get the fuel running through the clear plastic tube kept in the stern locker for the purpose.

'Be careful not to suck down a lungful,' he said. 'That's bad news, though less of a pain than accidentally siphoning a can full of water instead of petrol into the tank, which I've seen done. Always check the can is full of the right stuff.'

I did that carefully, and I'd finished the refuelling without spilling a drop, and stowed the canisters carefully, and double-checked everything else was ready to go, by the time Amelia and Xander strolled up. They were laughing about something they'd seen en route, but I was obviously giving off the wrong vibe and they didn't share the joke with me.

'Finally,' I said under my breath as they climbed aboard.

Pete exchanged a look with the others as if to say, 'What's got into him?'

Xander shrugged minutely in response.

To buoy up the mood, Pete explained the plan as we pootled out of the bay. He even went as far as to make it sound like he approved of where we were going now, but of course Amelia called him out with, 'But yesterday you told us it was a sub-standard place to search, probability-of-success-wise.'

'I've thought about it some more,' he said and left it at that. We'd reached the edge of the go-slow zone, so he let *Thunderbolt* do the rest of the talking by opening up her outboards.

The prow lifted and the hull rose with it, pinning us back in our seats for a moment. Then we were flying, the engines a-roar, the great white speedboat slapping the tops of the waves. Wind tugged at my hair and made my eyes stream. I looked behind us at the sea unzipping itself in our boiling wake.

After a time, the noise and vibrations of the outboards and the rushing wind and the juddering of the waves through the hull had a numbing effect on me and I forgot why I was annoyed. Excitement at what we might turn up built in me, blotting out everything else.

To conserve fuel, we cruised the last twenty or so minutes at a slower and more restful pace. The island rose up to meet us. There wasn't much of it. We puttered round to a beach, a little horseshoe of brilliant white, with arms extending into the sea as if in welcome.

Though the beach was deserted for now, Pete dropped anchor at a respectful distance. The sea was calm here and so blue it looked like somebody had photoshopped it. Behind the palm trees fronting the beach a slab-like grey building sat impassively. Slices of sunlight glanced off the waves and bounced back at us from the building's tinted windows. Other than that, nothing seemed to be moving.

'Somebody's a James Bond fan,' said Xander.

'It's completely out of keeping,' I replied.

'With what, exactly? It's the only thing here,' said Amelia.

'Fair point, but still.'

'Let's get going then,' I said, rolling up my wetsuit top, ramming my arms through the sleeves and reaching behind me for the zipper-string.

'Aye aye, captain,' said Xander, doing it up for me.

I could tell the others were as keen as me to make a start now, no doubt fuelled by thoughts of what we might find. A sense of urgency had set in. Amelia checked her oxygen, regulator, BCD and detector over with military precision, and Xander followed suit.

Within minutes we were underwater, three abreast, finning

our way purposefully to the western tip of the horseshoe. Once there, we slowed right down. The drill was to sweep each new site methodically rather than crisscross all over the place like headless underwater chickens.

A cloud of tiny orange fish, sparks flung from an angle-grinder, shot past us as we started, and the familiar chirruping soundtrack of our detectors at work heightened the hope I felt in that moment. It was an addictive feeling, that sense of possibility, the outside chance we might turn up something *big*.

9.

As it turned out, we had a slow start, by which I mean we didn't find anything all morning. For our first afternoon dive we worked the shallows and uncovered a Coke can. I didn't want to settle for that, obviously, so pressured Pete to let us go down one last time and strayed deeper than I should have, dragging the others with me. More idiotically still, when they surfaced I stayed down for an extra few minutes, then came up too fast to make up for it, breaking about six basic diver's rules. Pete was putting on his own kit to come down and look for me when I bobbed up next to the boat. Furious, he tore his mask off and threw it at me in the water.

'Never. Dive. Alone!' he shouted.

'I lost track . . . I . . .'

Neither Xander nor Amelia would look at me; both knew I was lying.

'And messing with the timings like that. It's all calculated carefully, to avoid you getting ill. We've been through it. Decompression sickness is a serious thing.'

'It was just a few minutes,' I mumbled.

'Doesn't matter.'

'It does, in fact,' said Amelia. 'The risk depends upon depth and time; it's not an on-and-off thing.'

She was right, we all knew that, but Pete's simple point – and the calculations he'd done – were designed to eliminate the risk, not just minimise it.

I'd been an idiot. That, combined with the general disappointment of the day, cast me into a truly black mood. There I was, with my two best friends, in paradise pretty much, with a haul of treasure back at the hotel already, and I'd somehow managed to make myself feel as grimly wrong as that streak of darkness on the blue horizon behind us.

Was I imagining it? No. There was a dot of a boat, with a wisp of smoke above it, in the distance to our stern. Amelia was inspecting her fingertips. Xander had his eyes shut, face turned to the lowering sun. And Pete was focused on one thing alone: getting us home.

'Guys,' I said through gritted teeth.

Xander turned to me.

'Look.'

'At what?'

'Is that what I think it is?'

'You'll have to say what you think it is for us to judge that,' said Amelia.

'Fire,' I said, loudly enough for Pete to hear.

He shot a look over his shoulder at me. 'What's that?'

'He's right,' said Xander. 'There, off to our left. Smoke?'

'Without which . . .' said Amelia.

Pete throttled back to idle and swung the boat round. He pulled a pair of binoculars from a compartment down by his knees, brought them up to his face and looked through them for a fair few seconds before muttering one word: 'Odd.'

'What's odd?' said Amelia.

Pete still had the binoculars pressed to his eyes. 'That boat was in the vicinity when you were down below. During your last dive it went past at a distance, quite slowly. Seems it circled the island. Now it's coming towards us, and it's smoking, you're right. But I can't see flames.'

'Do I have to repeat myself?' Amelia asked. 'There's no smoke without –'

'Yes, yes, I know but –'

'It's more bad than odd,' I said. 'We should get over there and help them.'

Pete had reached that conclusion too, it seemed, but reluctantly. He wasn't rushing. Maybe because I wanted to claw something back having let myself down, I snapped, 'Their boat's on fire. We need to help them *now*.'

Pete eased the throttle forward. He'd put down the binoculars. I picked them up and looked through them. It was hard to keep the image steady, but despite our bouncing I could make out a cabin cruiser trailing a plume of smoke. And there, on the bow, was a figure. He was slight. A boy, in fact. A small black boy waving something above his head, a flag, or T-shirt perhaps; I couldn't make it out.

Our boat glanced off a wave lip at that moment and I stopped looking through the binoculars.

'There's a kid on board,' I shouted over the noise of the engines. In response they grew louder. We bore down on the stricken boat. Since it was still somehow motoring towards us as well, the distance between the two boats shrank very rapidly indeed. In no time at all Pete was slackening off and we were dropping low into the water and I could clearly see that the little boy was waving a dirty beach towel. His eyes were very wide, the whites visible all around his dark irises.

The towel wasn't the only thing that was dirty, I noticed. The cabin cruiser's hull was grey and patched, and one half of the split windscreen had been replaced with a bit of board. The man piloting the boat was half hidden by it. For a horrible moment it seemed the two boats – our sleek weapon of a dive launch, long and low in the water, and the smoking, battered cruiser bobbing above us – might actually run into one another, but with a deft flick of his wrist Pete jinked left at the last minute, so that we drifted very slowly alongside the cruiser.

'Something's not right about this,' muttered Pete.

At precisely that moment, with the boats at a virtual standstill beside one another, two men leaped up above the cabin cruiser's rail. Each had a machine gun. The sea around us exploded with foam as both men unleashed a stream of bullets into the depths.

10.

A switch flipped inside me, flooding every muscle with exactly what it needed to answer the question: fight or flight? But there was nowhere to run to and nobody close enough to punch. Why on earth hadn't Pete hit the throttles? No idea. He'd put his hands above his head instead.

'Go!' I shouted, and lunged forward to get us out of there myself.

Before I made it to the controls the gunman nearest us let loose again, inches above *Thunderbolt*'s prow at first, but then he delivered a second microburst that actually hit us, ripping bits of fibreglass from the immaculate white hood.

In the quiet that followed this volley the man who fired it raised an arm, signalling for us to put ours up. He was still waving his semi-automatic haphazardly in our direction with his free hand.

'Do as he says,' hissed Pete.

My heart was jack-hammering in my chest. I lifted my

hands. Xander and Amelia did the same. She looked ashen and he was panting with fear.

Smoke was still billowing from the rear of the battered cruiser, a black column rising above us. It didn't seem to be hampering the captain though. We were drifting forward, but he had put the cruiser in reverse and was matching our speed, the prow nosing closer to ours as we went.

As soon as the gap between the two boats was jumpable the kid who'd been waving the towel leaped. He'd lost the rag now, and was instead holding the end of a length of rope. The boy was barefoot and wearing cut-off jeans. In no time at all he'd worked that rope through an eyelet on the prow and tied it off expertly.

The launch, lashed to us now, swung round to reveal its stern. A low, shelf-like platform stuck out of the back of the boat a couple of feet above the water line. In the middle of this shelf stood an oil drum, the source of the smoke, pouring upwards into the sky.

A third man, every fine muscle in his arms and chest seemingly visible beneath his smooth black skin, pushed the barrel off the shelf with a single kick. It flopped forward, spilling flame and tar into the turquoise sea.

That act, the casual selfishness of it, scared me even more than the crack of bullets splitting fibreglass. It made me think of Mum. Her selfless campaign to protect Zanzibar's coral reef was so at odds with what this man had just done, I felt physically sick.

No doubt the fear coursing through me made the sensation worse. From where I was standing, I could see the barrel

47

sink through the clear water beneath us, sludge unrolling from it as it went.

What had I done?

If I hadn't insisted otherwise, we'd have stayed close to the main islands of the archipelago, rather than sailing all the way up here. If I hadn't insisted otherwise, we'd have left more than an hour ago, and we'd be safely back at Ras Nungwi about now. If I hadn't insisted otherwise, we wouldn't have fallen for the boat-in-distress smoke signal that Pete had been suspicious of; we'd have turned around at a distance and outrun the guns easily. If I hadn't insisted otherwise, Pete's precious speedboat wouldn't now be overrun with thieves.

I thought of Mum. She'd lost her eldest son to a stupid accident caused by me. I'd also uncovered her husband's terrible deceit. She'd thought him a good man until I'd effectively pulled the mask from his face. After I did so he was dead to her too. And now I'd gone and got myself kidnapped by pirates. Mum is a tough woman but this would break her. With the rest of our family dead or gone, we only had each other. I was scared for myself in those moments, but I was dying inside for Mum.

As well as the boy, the ripped guy who'd kicked the barrel into the sea was on board now. Both of them moved around the boat without speaking to us, while the men with the guns kept them trained our way from on high. Barrel-man seemed to be inspecting things. He picked up one of the detectors and looked it over with interest, then he put it back down carefully. Next, he had a little rummage through the stowed scuba gear. He looked a bit like a man browsing in a shop without any intention of actually buying anything.

'What do they want?' whispered Amelia.

Barrel-man overheard her and swivelled instantly. He took her in, an almost playful look on his face, then he looked me and Xander up and down as well, before his eyes eventually came to rest on Pete. For a second he stood still, as if considering something. Then he corralled the three of us kids, hands still raised, towards the stern.

In a language I didn't recognise he yelled something up at the cruiser while surveying the three of us in turn again. A voice from the boat shouted something back. It belonged to an older black guy wearing a baseball cap backwards who now emerged from the cabin and leaned over the rail to inspect what was down below. I felt like an exhibit in a zoo.

The two men carried on their conversation. They seemed to be disagreeing about something. The captain had the final say, or at least he ended the conversation by looking from Pete to us and back again before flicking his fingers dismissively. In response Barrel-man hopped over to Pete, gently eased the sunglasses from his face, and put them high on his own head.

Pete blinked at him. Veins stood out in his muscled neck.

A trickle of sweat ran down between my shoulder blades.

Absurdly, I hoped the answer to Amelia's question – what do they want? – may be just that: Pete's sunglasses. Nothing more. Barrel-man had done his browsing and, having looked through everything we had on display, that's

49

what he'd chosen. Perhaps he would offer to pay for them. He might even want a receipt?

I knew none of that was true just as well as I knew it was all my fault. I'd as good as invited these men aboard. Pirates. Come on in, have a look around, take what you want. Barrel-man would have the sunglasses for good measure, sure, but he'd have the rest as well.

11.

Since the situation was my fault, it was up to me to do something about it. But what? Pete had told me to do what these guys wanted. Barrel-man, Pete's sunglasses still balanced on his forehead – why didn't he wear them properly, given the brilliant sunset? – had now come upon our dry-bags, hung from hooks on the bulwark. He went through Amelia's first, pulled out her sunscreen, dropped it back in, held up a T-shirt and did the same with that, then found her phone, inspected it, and slid that back into the bag as well.

Did that mean he might return it to her? No, it was still far more likely that he planned to have it all. He went through my and Xander's bags next. He was so unhurried and deliberate in his movements. I don't have to make a show here, he seemed to be saying: you're powerless, so I can do exactly what I want.

Watching this thug go through our stuff was tough, but at least the rings we'd found at the bottom of the ocean weren't there for him to discover. Amelia had taken all of

51

them to look after the previous night, so they were locked in her room safe back at the hotel, but I held my breath as the guy went through her stuff all the same. When he didn't take anything, I breathed out slowly. It was a silver lining of sorts.

I cast about for something – anything – to upset the imbalance of power. The boy was still in our boat, sitting comfortably on the gunwale near us, one thin leg across the other, showing me the pink sole of his foot. There were white cracks across it. He reached down and scratched his shin, eyes alert, dancing from the men with guns to Barrel-man to the captain, Pete and us. When he next looked my way I caught his gaze and tried to hold it by doing something he wouldn't expect, namely smiling.

He smiled in return.

There was a big gap between his bright white front teeth.

I nodded at him.

He nodded back.

Unable to think of anything else to do, I murmured, 'You OK?'

'Better than you, I expect,' he replied.

I fought a double take but both Xander and Amelia beside me, hearing the boy speak English, looked up at him in surprise.

'You're right, I've been better,' I said.

'Stay calm. That's my advice,' the boy replied, still smiling.

'What's your name?' asked Xander.

'Mo,' he replied, eyes darting from us to the others. 'Yours?'

'Xander.'

'I've not heard that name before, where's it from?'

'Nowhere in particular, but it's short for Alexander,' said Xander conversationally.

'Ah,' said the boy. 'I'm from Somalia. We all are.'

Under her breath Amelia said, 'Great, pirates from Somalia. Just great.'

To head off the potential insult of Amelia's sarcasm Xander said, 'This is Amelia, and that's Jack.'

'Xander, Amelia and Jack,' the boy said. 'I'm still Mo.'

'Yes, obviously,' said Amelia under her breath.

The boy, Mo, had sharp ears. He not only repeated what Amelia had said, but did so in her London accent. 'Yes, obviously.' Speaking like that made me realise that his own accent was a bit American. Nothing was adding up.

Barrel-man, cottoning on to the noise of this conversation if not its meaning, turned to tell Mo something that was at once unintelligible to me and yet obvious, along the lines of 'Shut up!'

I was watching Pete out of the corner of my eye. The sweat was pouring off him now. His hands, which he'd been holding high, had inched down to his chest. He kept looking from the deck of the cruiser to Barrel-man and back again.

One of the gunmen was speaking over his shoulder to the wheelhouse. Pete's right hand dropped lower still. Was he about to do something? Mo must also have been watching the divemaster, thinking what I was, because he said, 'I'd tell your boss to be sensible if I was you. He may be a good swimmer, but he won't get far with a bullet in his head.'

53

Barrel-man took two quick steps towards Mo, yelling whatever 'shut up' was again as he went, and slapped him across the face. That slap would have knocked me off the gunwale, but Mo somehow took it. He swayed there before Barrel-man, staring at the deck.

With the pirate's back turned, Pete lunged after him. He caught a shoulder with one hand and locked his other forearm across Barrel-man's neck, spun, and held him as a human shield.

The ex-soldier was much the bigger of the two men, his sunburnt shoulder twice the size of the pirate's, but amazingly Barrel-man, all sinew and muscle, wriggled out of Pete's neck lock with apparent ease.

As well as being stronger, he was nimbler. Before either of the gunmen on the boat had bothered to train their weapons on the pair, Barrel-man, having slipped Pete's grip, had somehow grabbed him by the throat and marched him to the side of the boat. He had Pete unbalanced there. The dive master was on one leg, his hip against the fibreglass.

I was too slow. By the time I realised what was happening – that Barrel-man was actually pushing Pete overboard – I couldn't do anything to stop it. Pete slip-fell into the water with the same harmless splash we all did at the start of a dive. And immediately the speedboat, tugged gently by the cruiser, swung away from him, opening up a few feet of water, ten, fifteen, twenty. Though Pete kicked after us, he couldn't close the gap.

Amelia was shouting at Mo, something about throwing out a rope. Perhaps Mo knew better than to respond. I couldn't stop myself though. There was no rope within easy reach but I knew about the life jackets stowed beneath the bench seat the three of us were sitting on, and before anyone could object I flung one out over the stern. Pete, still making after us, gathered it in.

The man in the wheelhouse had come out next to the gunmen again, and as before he seemed to be angry, this time at the guy who'd raised his rifle to his shoulder and was pointing it at Pete. It was obvious that the gunman wanted to pull the trigger. I couldn't tell if the captain was urging him to get it over with or to lower his gun.

'Mo, please,' I begged. 'Tell them not to do it. Let us throw out a rope and pull Pete in.'

Mo looked the other way. It was as if he could no longer understand me. For an awful moment I thought: he knows what's coming next.

12.

The gunman on the cruiser, assault rifle pulled into his shoulder, cheek pressed tight to the stock, had one eye shut and the other unblinkingly open, staring straight over the sight at Pete in the water. He definitely wanted to pull the trigger.

Barrel-man wanted the same thing: he was shouting from the speedboat to do it. But the captain from the wheelhouse, the older guy who'd been piloting the cruiser, had one hand raised steadily aloft now. Was he about to give the order? Mercifully, no: he was holding the man back, his raised hand a stop sign, saying, don't waste bullets.

All the while the boats were drifting further away from Pete. He'd got his right arm through the life jacket. As I watched, he worked his left hand through the other loop and, kicking onto his back, fastened the vest across his chest.

He was no longer trying to reach us. We were already more than the length of a swimming pool away from him. The red of the jacket merged into the darker red of Pete's face as we moved still further away.

Barrel-man, angry at having been rushed by Pete, seemed to want more in the way of revenge. He stalked over to me. I braced myself. But he didn't hit me as he had hit the boy, Mo. Instead he dropped to his haunches, yanked a handful of life jackets from the compartment under the bench seat and threw them at us. He shouted at us then but of course I couldn't understand him.

'Mo?' said Xander.

'He says to put them on,' Mo, still on the gunwale, said, adding, 'but I wouldn't if I were you.'

Barrel-man shouted at us again, homing in on me. The whites of his eyes had a yellowish tinge and the anger pulsed from him. He picked up one of the life jackets and swung it at my face. I ducked and raised an arm to protect myself and somehow ended up holding on to the thing.

From the cruiser I could hear the captain, still arguing with his men. It seemed Barrel-man thought I should be punished for throwing Pete a life jacket identical to the one I was now holding, and although I couldn't understand him precisely it was obvious enough what he thought my punishment should be.

If I did as he wanted, and jumped overboard wearing the life jacket, I'd at least be in – or rather out of – the same boat as Pete. Didn't I deserve as much? I'm ashamed to say I just stood there, my face a mask of I-don't-know-what-to-do.

Beside me, Xander bent slowly to pick up a life jacket. Amelia did the same. None of us put them on; we just stood there before Barrel-man holding the life jackets to our chests, as if they might offer us some sort of protection from him.

Barrel-man had backed off an inch or two. Up on the cabin cruiser's rail the captain was talking more softly, and both gunmen had lowered their weapons. Meanwhile Pete was a dot in the distance, rising and falling with the gentle swell. A seabird flapped lazily between us and him, underlining the ever-widening gap.

Pete had made the mistake of challenging one of the pirates and they were teaching us all a lesson. That's what this had to be, this gentle chugging towards the horizon: a scare tactic, all for show. Any moment now we would circle back to pick him up, wouldn't we? I looked to Mo again and said, 'We're going back for him, right?' but he didn't even turn my way.

The captain tossed something down to Barrel-man. It was a roll of gaffer tape. He caught it one-handed and came for me first, ripped the life jacket from me and threw it into the hold, then pushed me back down onto the bench and wrapped a length of tape around my ankles very tightly indeed.

There was no point resisting. I let him guide my hands behind my back and sat still while he bound my wrists together in the same way. He muttered to himself as he did this, and leaning across me I caught the smell of him, not the tang of sweat I'd been expecting but a weird mixture of diesel and soap.

When he was satisfied that I was safely trussed up he set to shackling Xander and Amelia in the same way. Xander followed my lead and made no fuss, but Amelia couldn't hold back. As he yanked the tape tight around her wrists she said, 'Ow! It doesn't need to be that tight to be effective!'

By now the boy, Mo, had moved to the speedboat's prow, and following instructions from the captain he hauled on the rope connecting the two boats until we were close enough for the captain to climb down over the side of the cruiser onto *Thunderbolt*'s long white hood. As well as his backwards baseball cap he was wearing a mismatched military-style outfit, a shirt with epaulettes on the shoulders and khaki trousers full of cargo pockets. Also, bright white Adidas trainers.

Unlike Barrel-man and the boy, who flitted about the speedboat with gymnastic ease, the captain moved stiffly, as if he had a bad back or was carrying some other injury. He inspected his prize with interest, tapping the fuel gauge and running a hand over the immaculate white armrest of Pete's seat, looking over everything methodically.

'Good,' he said with a smile. 'Good, yes? Good!'

13.

Within minutes Pete was out of sight. We were sailing away from him. At no great rate, just bubbling along, but making headway all the same. The slim line of the island soon dropped below the horizon behind us. Treasure-hunting: could anything, given what had just happened, seem more purposeless?

I tried to make myself believe Pete would be able to swim back to the island, but deep down I knew the reality of the currents sweeping through the Zanzibar archipelago; Pete had warned us about them himself. Why hadn't I thought to throw him a pair of fins as well as the life jacket?

I couldn't stop thinking of what Pete must be going through out there, alone at sea. Having just spent so many hours swimming in it I knew all too well that sensation of bobbing among the waves after surfacing from a dive.

With his eyes just an inch or two above the shifting lid of the sea his sense of his own insignificance would be amplified horribly. Practically speaking, being so low in the water would make it harder for Pete to catch sight of land than it was for me now, just a few feet above the surface, on the boat.

Though I was safe here with my friends the thought of Pete out there left me so desperate that for a long while panic overshadowed the tingling in my arms and growing numbness in the fingers of my left hand. Safe?! What was I thinking? We'd been overrun by pirates.

Amelia's description, back in the hotel, of the terrible conflict fought by child soldiers in Somalia rang in my ears now. These guys were desperate and ruthless. We weren't 'safe' at all! I was surprised to find myself straining against the gaffer tape, more so when Mo arrived at my side to check the binding.

'Let him go,' he murmured. 'You can do nothing to help.'

'What did you say?' I said, though I knew full well, and hated him for it.

'Does this hurt?' he asked, taking hold of the makeshift handcuffs, pinching the tape, twisting it.

I didn't want to give him the satisfaction of admitting that it did, but I couldn't help flinching.

'Here, let me,' he said, and having found the end of the tape he unpicked it and unwound it before wrapping my wrists together again more loosely.

Barrel-man saw what Mo was doing and flitted across the deck to inspect his work, the tone of whatever he was saying a clear threat: make sure that it's still tight enough to do the job!

Mo reassured him evenly. To me he whispered, as if we

were having a normal conversation, 'What's it called again, the flow of blood?'

'Circulation,' said Amelia. 'You can restore mine too if you like.'

Mo obliged, re-taping Amelia's wrists. 'This is just a caution, until they feel they can trust you.'

'Precaution,' said Amelia. 'And who is this "they"?'

'OK, "we" if you want. But they did the same to me.'

'They stole your boat too?' said Xander. He clearly wanted to keep the chat going. I didn't; I wanted the kid to go away. But I knew Xander was probably right to keep him talking.

Mo laughed softly. 'No. They didn't find me on a boat like this.'

Xander shifted so that he didn't have to address Mo over his shoulder. 'Where did they find you then?'

'At home.'

'Home?'

'What was left of it.'

'Where was that, then?'

Mo shrugged. 'You won't have heard of the place.'

'Try me,' Amelia said.

'A small village near Rassini.'

I could tell she desperately wanted to claim she'd heard of this Rassini place, but Amelia doesn't lie. The best she could do was say nothing.

'In Lower Juba.'

Still no joy.

'Somalia, very far –'

'South,' Amelia said quickly.

'Yes,' said Mo, looking at her askance.

'Near the border with Kenya,' she said. 'Historically the region either side of that border has been contested. Typical post-colonial bodge job. The line between the two countries was drawn by the British when they handed back control of their territories in the region.'

'They?' said Mo.

Amelia gave him almost exactly the same sideways glance he'd given her. I didn't expect you to clock that, it said.

'OK, we,' she conceded. 'If you don't mind my saying, you don't sound entirely Somali.'

Aping her accent with uncanny precision, Mo said, 'If you don't mind my saying, you do sound entirely British.'

'That's because I am,' said Amelia matter-of-factly.

Having finished adjusting our bindings, Mo was now squatting beside us. Again I caught sight of the fissures across the pale soles of his feet. This whole getting-to-know-you thing, fascinating though it was, did not stop me wanting to pick him up and throw him overboard. At least Pete stood a chance of swimming back to the island; there was no way this Mo fellow could have managed it. He deserved to sink. And yet obviously he wasn't calling the shots. Neither was the guy who deserved to drown most of all, Barrel-man. He'd actually tipped poor Pete out. And now he was sitting up front in Pete's seat, as if he owned the speedboat himself, all sinew and muscle etched by the low sun.

When I got my chance I'd make him pay for what he'd done to my friend. But the real culprit, the mastermind behind this act of piracy, was the older guy with the stupid white trainers and mismatched uniform. He was in charge. He'd already climbed back up to the wheelhouse of the bigger boat. It was towing us more purposefully now, at a greater distance, somebody aboard it having once again lengthened the rope that connected us.

The sun was dropping toward the horizon off to our left, meaning we were making our way north. My geography's nothing like as good as Amelia's, but I understood enough to know the mainland coast lay that way. A slice of Tanzania, then the strip of Kenyan coastline, with the great length of Somalia above it. Where were these guys taking us? What did they want with a supercharged speedboat and three random kids?

14.

If you want to know the answer to a question it's often a good tactic to ask it. Though I didn't want to talk to him, Mo was still sitting at the back of the boat with us, not guarding us as such – we were still tied up, so there was no real need – but keeping an eye on us while pretending to hang out.

Xander and Amelia might be content to exchange pleasantries with him, but I wanted to know what was going on. So I cut across Xander, who was explaining how he was half Nigerian, and said, 'What's the point of this?'

'This?' said Mo.

'Stealing the boat, kidnapping us, murdering our friend.'

'Nobody murdered anybody,' said Mo quietly.

'As good as,' I spat.

'I tried to warn you. These are ruthless men.'

'I can see that. But what do they want?'

'Isn't it obvious? They want this boat.'

'What for?'

'It's a valuable boat. Also useful. It's very fast.'

'Useful for what?'

If I'd been able to move I'd have wiped the look Mo gave me in response to that question clean off his face. It was a look that said, Can you work nothing out for yourself? As if explaining the rules of tag to a pre-schooler, he said, 'These men are pirates. They make their living by taking valuable things from other people at sea. To do that they have many strategies. Tricking boats to come close is one tactic. That worked with you guys. But mostly it doesn't. So usually they rely on speed. For that they need fast boats. Their last skiff sank three weeks ago in a storm. They need another. With her –' he pointed at the battered cruiser – 'they can go far, but not fast. With this boat,' he tapped *Thunderbolt*'s fibreglass hull, 'With this boat they can hunt at speed.'

A bank of cloud lay on the horizon behind Mo. As he gave this explanation the sun edged below the cloud and its soft white underbelly was serrated with copper and gold. It looked artificial, perfect as a painting. Mo was briefly silhouetted. If the painter had been responsible for him too, the boy would have been the saint in the scene.

'But what about us?' asked Xander quietly.

'Don't worry,' Mo replied. 'It will be OK.'

'That's not an answer,' said Amelia bluntly.

Mo nodded. 'True,' he said. 'But it's supposed to be better than one.'

'How?'

'It's called reassurance.'

Amelia gave him her that-doesn't-compute look. He

seemed to understand it, respect it almost. Logic would reassure Amelia, nothing less. 'You are not in danger,' he went on. 'Not if you do what they say. You are valuable, like the boat. More so, in fact. They will want to trade you in, not waste you. You don't even need to do anything! You have value just by being you. Unlike . . .'

'Unlike what?' said Amelia.

I was ahead of her for once. It wasn't a 'what' Mo was getting at, but a 'who'. I think he'd stopped short of saying it because he knew it would sound a bit self-pitying. Obviously the 'who' was him. And yes, I was right. Though he was trying to head off the poor-little-me stuff by sounding cheerful now, it didn't work. With a smile he said, 'Unlike me.'

He was pathetic. I hated him for it. But Amelia just wanted to know the specifics. Ignoring – or not even noticing, perhaps – that he'd regretted making the comparison and tried not to follow through with it, she asked, 'What's so worthless about you?'

'I didn't say I was worthless.'

'Non-valuable then.'

'I said I wasn't worth a lot to them just by being me.'

'Why not?'

'I don't have anybody who'd pay a lot of money to get me back. They're betting you do.'

There and then I made a decision. Whatever happened, I'd do my best to make sure these guys didn't get a reward by demanding a ransom for our release. I didn't know how I'd do it, but I'd find a way. I'd spite them. Given what had happened to Mum in the DRC, with Langdon paying himself a fake ransom not to free Mum and Dad, I'd been put off the idea of paying kidnappers for good. It hadn't worked then and it wouldn't work now because I wasn't about to let it.

'I wouldn't be so sure of that,' I said.

Mo didn't bother replying to me. He could probably sense Amelia wasn't done with him yet.

'How did you make yourself non-worthless then?' she asked.

'I had to work at it.'

'How?'

'By becoming useful.'

'Any idiot can tie a knot in a rope or wrap someone's hands in gaffer tape,' I said.

Mo nodded and said, 'I meant learning English, but you'd be surprised; some people find knots tricky.'

Xander's always quick to sniff out bullshit, even if he hides his incredulity behind good humour. Smiling now, he said, 'You learned English to help a pirate gang. That's likely. What did they do, enrol you in a language school, pay for lessons?'

Mo smiled back at him. 'No. But they let me go online every now and then, and also watch foreign movies. *Fast and Furious. Jason Bourne.* That sort of thing.'

'You expect us to believe you learned to speak fluent English by watching a few action films?' Xander laughed. 'That's totally likely.'

Mo just shrugged.

Amelia, hunched uncomfortably because of her bound

hands, was looking at Mo strangely. I'd seen the look before, but only once or twice. There was this time a kid two years younger than her beat her in a massive chess competition in London. I'd gone along to support her. Halfway through the match she realised she'd been outplayed, and when that realisation dawned on her she looked both stunned and strangely pleased, her annoyance blindsided by admiration. Now, out of nowhere, she asked, 'What colour is anhydrous copper sulphate?'

'White.'

'What colour does it go when you hydrate it?'

'Blue.'

'And what's the chemical formula for hydrated copper sulphate?'

'$CuSO_4.5H_2O$.'

Without missing a beat Amelia went on, 'Who was Hitler's minister for propaganda?'

'Joseph Goebbels.'

'What month did he die?'

'He died the day after Hitler, on May 1st 1945.'

'What's the relationship between the pressure and temperature of a gas in a rigid container?'

'Constant,' Mo said quietly.

'Assuming what?'

'Assuming that temperature is measured in Kelvin,' Mo added without looking up.

Amelia drew breath to fire another question at Mo, and I reckon she'd have stumped him eventually if she'd kept going, but she let the breath out without trying.

Xander, who'd been listening quietly, said, 'Do you speak any more languages, other than Somali and English?'

Mo nodded. 'A few.'

Xander puffed out his cheeks. 'And you learned all this how again?'

'I just sort of picked it up.'

'Oh come on,' said Xander. I felt the same way. I'd been learning French for six years, could barely ask the way to the shops, and definitely wouldn't understand the answer. But I was watching Amelia, and everything about her face said she believed this boy, Mo. She'd know, I suppose. If it was possible, my hatred of him ratcheted up another notch. Xander hadn't clocked Amelia's reaction. He said, 'You really expect us to believe that?'

Mo shrugged again.

'Where'd you learn it all really?'

'Here and there, like I said.'

'The chemical formula for whatever just hopped into your head, did it?'

He rolled his scrawny shoulders and looked away uncomfortably. 'What does it matter? I know stuff. Most of it's useless. But some of it helps me, and if you let me I can use it to help you.'

I realised I'd been clenching my fists together, pumping them full of blood within their gaffer-tape manacles. They hurt. All the same, if they'd been taped together in front of me, then even despite my taped ankles I'd have risked toppling flat on my face to lurch in the boy's direction, use them like a club, and see whether I could whack him out

70

of the boat with them. I wasn't falling for this 'let me help you' stuff, not at all. But my hands were behind my back and anyway, Mo had scuttled off to the speedboat's prow, called there by the captain, who'd descended to the rear platform of the battered cruiser to have a word with him. What he was ordering the boy to do now, God alone knew.

15.

'What's the plan?' Xander asked once Mo was out of earshot.

I didn't have one, but I couldn't tell him that. 'I'll think of something. For now we sit tight and –'

'We don't have much choice about that,' muttered Amelia.

'– and observe things,' I went on. 'Let's see what these guys do and work out their weak link. One thing is for sure, I'm not putting my trust in that Mo.'

'Why not?' asked Amelia.

'The fact that he knows the chemical formula for Hitler's propagandist, or whatever, doesn't impress me. They're just using him to keep us quiet. I wouldn't trust him further than I could throw him.'

Xander shifted beside me. He didn't say anything, but the way he didn't meet my eye made it clear enough that Mo seemed all right to him. Normally I'd have been swayed by that; Xander has amazing instincts around people. But today I felt myself tense up defiantly. 'He did nothing to help Pete,' I said under my breath.

'What could he have done?' said Amelia.

'Objected! Got in the way! Pulled the guy off him!'

'None of us did any of those things,' she pointed out.

'We had a gun pointed at us,' said Xander, trying to keep the peace.

'True,' replied Amelia. 'But if what he says is true, then logical extrapolation means he did too.'

'Big "if",' I said.

Amelia's face made it clear she thought I had no idea.

'What do you think of Pete's chances . . . out there?' said Xander.

'He's a strong swimmer and he knows the currents.' My heart wasn't in this reply.

Amelia didn't exactly make matters better with her own answer to Xander's question: 'Impossible to gauge the probability of him making a successful sea swim without more detail.' Seeing my head drop she continued, 'Although you're right that his swimming prowess increases the chance of a positive outcome.'

'Poor guy,' said Xander quietly.

I shook my head but it did nothing to dislodge the worry. 'Yes,' I whispered. 'Poor guy.'

A gentle breeze had sprung up, drawing ripples across the slow-moving sea. The water wasn't turquoise any more, but indigo cut with orange. The sun had dipped below the horizon and now the sky above us loomed very empty indeed. It would be dark soon.

Where were they taking us? I had no idea. And why tow the boat when it was perfectly capable of propelling itself?

I was annoyed by the realisation that there was only one person I could ask, namely Mo. He'd disappeared into the wheelhouse of the cabin cruiser with the captain, and now emerged wearing a battered backpack. The cruiser slowed. In no time he'd hauled in the line and skipped between the two boats again.

He ran the length of the hood and jumped lightly down onto the bench, nimbly sidestepping the dive gear strapped in the hold. When he reached us, he sat down. He was smiling. I glowered back. He swung his rucksack into his lap and opened it up, asking, 'Are you thirsty? Hungry? Here, the captain sends you some food and drinks.'

I turned away from him, but Amelia said, 'What sort of food?'

He was rummaging about in his bag and spoke into it. '*Kimis*, a flat type of bread, and here, some *mukmaad*, which is dried-out beef.'

'Jerky,' said Xander.

Mo broke the word in half, trying it out: 'Jerk key. Also, mango,' he said, holding one up.

'I'm not hungry,' I told him.

'Drink though,' he said, holding up a plastic bottle beaded with droplets. It looked like it had come out of a fridge.

In silence I let him hold the bottle to my lips, knowing that without water I'd weaken in a matter of hours. The instant before he tilted the bottle, I realised I was parched, but when I took the first gulp I almost spat it out in surprise. The clear, bubbly liquid wasn't water but lemonade. It felt like a trick. I couldn't stop myself drinking some more all the same.

74

'It's good, yes?' he said.

I turned away from him again.

He helped the others to drink and fed them as well, tearing off chunks of the flatbread and jerky and posting the pieces into Amelia and Xander's open mouths. How demeaning, to be fed like a baby. I was glad I'd refused, but knowing they had eaten I immediately felt horribly hungry. I'd have to cave in soon, I supposed, but for now it felt good to have taken a stand.

Mo was apologising for the fact we were tied up. 'It's just until they can trust you,' he said. 'I will try to convince them, first thing in the morning, when it's light.'

'But where are we sleeping?' asked Amelia.

The whites of Mo's eyes were bright in the gloom. He looked apologetically into the hold. 'We can use the life jackets to make things a little more comfortable,' he said. 'And there are blankets on the big boat. I will ask for some. I can't promise, but let's see.'

Without waiting for a response, he set off. The speed at which he left did make it look like he felt guilty and genuinely wanted to help, but it could have been an act. And again, when he returned with the promised blankets under his arm, he seemed proud to have negotiated them for us successfully, but for all I knew the captain had already told him to give them to us. I wasn't about to follow Xander's ever-so-grateful act, though I had to admit that keeping the boy onside was probably a good thing.

Now Mo was pulling out the life jackets and spreading them across the bottom of the boat. It wouldn't make much difference. None of us would get any sleep with our hands tied behind our backs. Still, Amelia was shuffling herself into a more comfortable position, evidently ready to make the most of Mo's efforts, and Xander allowed him to drape a blanket over his shoulders.

The dark came so quickly. What was left of the sunset drained away and the cloudbank became a black lid that slowly slid to one side over the next hour or so, revealing a night sky stabbed full of more stars than I'd seen before in my life. Unlike at home, where even the most starlit night sky looks like a single black sheet full of pinpricks of light, the sky above the boat was full of depth, with some stars so distant they were barely visible and others seemingly near enough to touch.

Barrel-man had his feet up on the boat's dashboard, to one side of the steering wheel. He was leaning back in Pete's chair, dozing. Astonishingly, Mo's efforts to make things tolerable for us seemed to have paid off for Amelia. She was curled up on her side at my feet, breathing in the steady rhythm of sleep. And before long Mo, cocooned in his blanket, seemed to have drifted off as well. But I was still electrically awake, and though his back was turned to me I could sense that Xander, like me, either didn't want to give in to sleep, or couldn't.

The burbling of the cruiser's motor, together with the slap and splash of water beneath our hull, was enough to mask a little noise, so I decided to risk it.

'Xander,' I whispered.

'Yes,' he breathed.

'Keep an eye on the pirate. If he stirs, do something to distract him. OK?'

'Sure.'

Very slowly indeed I twisted from a sitting position until I was curled on my side among the life jackets. Then, over the course of about fifteen minutes, I inched my way along the bottom of the boat towards the raised platform that supported Pete's chair. Not because I wanted to get at Barrel-man – what could I do with my hands bound? – but because I needed to reach the starboard bulwark behind his seat. Our dry-bags were hung on hooks there.

Fortunately, the closer I got to Barrel-man the less likely he was to see me; by the time I was pressed up behind the forward platform he would have had to turn right round and lean over his chair-back to spot me.

Still, I had the problem of unhitching my bag without it thumping down into the hold. The best I could think to do was to try and lift it from its hook with my feet and let it flop down onto my midriff, cushioning the bag's fall with my body.

That was the plan, but for long moments I couldn't manage it. To stop things bouncing off them in rough seas, the hooks had barbed lips. Try as I might, I couldn't manipulate the bag finely enough with my feet. A howl of frustration welled up within me. I fought to keep my cool, took a deep breath, tried for the bag again. There was a strange squeaking in my ears as I struggled with it, a noise I realised was coming from me, ferociously grinding my teeth.

Could I time it so that the bag fell when we hit a wave? No: there was no pattern to the background boat noise. Just get on with it, I told myself. What's the worst Barrel-man might do if he caught me? Trying to reassure myself with that question was pointless. He could chuck me overboard like Pete. Well, that was a risk I'd have to take. Holding my breath again, I finally levered the dry-bag clear of its hook, and let it slide-tumble down my leg and onto my chest.

Nothing happened. Specifically, no head appeared over the seat-back. I glanced across at Xander, plainly visible in the starlight. He nodded at me almost imperceptibly. So far, so good. The boat rose and fell to the same gentle soundtrack, the stars rocking from side to side above it.

With my back to the bulwark I eased myself up into a sitting position and shifted the dry-bag to my side. I had to strain to reach the clasp fastening its neck, but once I had hold of it I managed to pinch the thing apart easily enough. It didn't take me long to fish out my phone. Once I had it, I fastened the bag shut again and, lying on my back, I pushed it up to the bulwark again with my feet.

That part wasn't as tricky as it sounds. The carry handle slipped over the hook easily enough. Inching my way back to the stern was agony though. The night sky seemed to have grown brighter still. If Barrel-man had thought to check he would definitely have spotted me out of place. But he didn't, and soon enough I'd made it back to my slot between Amelia and Xander. She was still sleeping, but he was very much awake.

'What are you up to?' he whispered.

'I need to send a message,' I replied.

'To who? Saying what?'

'I'm going to tell Mum to blank these guys when they make contact asking for money.'

Xander shifted so that he could see my face close-up. 'You're going to do *what*?!'

'Trust me,' I whispered.

'You know I trust you, but . . .' He tailed off.

It was impossible to use my phone behind my back. No matter how much I strained, I couldn't see the screen while I was holding it. But I managed to ignite the thing blind and, sitting shoulder to shoulder with Xander, with him angling it my way, I could see it.

I always keep my phone on silent: only an idiot wants to be interrupted by constant notifications. That's why none of the rash of messages spread across its screen had made it beep or buzz. All of the messages were from Mum. The first, casual and breezy, asked when we expected to be back at the resort. When she'd received no reply, she'd sent further pleas for an update. Mum always punctuates and proofreads her texts carefully, but the last message she'd sent was a frantic *Please Jack pick up or reply I'm really so worried* without commas or a full stop at the end.

My heartbeat had slowed down since I'd retrieved the phone. Now it felt dead in my chest, a plodding boom of sadness for poor, poor Mum.

I knew what I wanted to tell Mum, and I knew how upset she'd be to hear it, but thinking up the right – few – words was nowhere near as hard as getting them typed. Very slowly indeed, I managed to write the message. There were two bars of signal when I started, but they had flickered down to one by the time I'd pecked out my simple *we're OK – don't pay ransom – trust me – i've got this –* message.

I was worried we'd slip out of range entirely if I went on any longer so I just added – *love j –* and hit send. The *delivered* confirmation seemed to take an age to come through, but it was probably just my imagination. Either way, I deleted the sent message, killed the phone screen and gave Xander a thank-you nod before rolling back onto my side with the phone clamped tight in my hand.

I'd been keeping an eye on both Barrel-man and Mo as I'd gone through this laborious process. Neither had moved. And yet, as I slid the phone under my life-jacket mattress, Mo, who had been lying on his back, shifted up onto one elbow. He didn't say anything, but in that moment he was definitely looking my way.

16.

Against all the odds I did sleep that night eventually. I don't remember drifting off but I must have because the next thing I knew I was coming to, plucking up the courage to open one eye, knowing exactly where I was and yet hoping I was mistaken and it had all been a bad dream.

No such luck.

Dawn was just about to break: the stars above me had faded as the deep black sky bleached to grey. I tried to lever myself upright but my arms were having none of it. They were beyond numb. When I tried to lean on my left elbow, I felt nothing at all.

Mo spotted me trying to wriggle some feeling back into myself. The boy was bouncing on his heels before us in a matter of seconds. I wouldn't have called on him, but I wasn't about to stand in the way of his help.

'I'll ask if we can untie you,' he said. 'One minute.'

With that he skipped forward to whisper in Barrel-man's ear. When he returned his smile made me momentarily hopeful he'd got permission to unbind us completely, but all he'd managed was to convince Barrel-man that we could be trusted to have our wrists taped together in front of us.

This he did, to Xander first. When my shoulders rolled forward for the first time in roughly half a day it felt like they were being ripped out of their sockets. I couldn't hold back a grunt of pain. Amelia, who had been asleep up until that moment, sat up. 'What's going on? Someone's hurt?' she asked.

I waited for the pain to kick in for her too, but amazingly she simply stretched her arms out behind her as if performing some sort of swimmer's warm-up exercise instead. She looked almost comfortable. When Mo redid her binding with her hands in her lap she seemed more confused than relieved. 'If it makes you happy,' she said.

While Mo had been attending to us I'd kept my position on top of the life jackets. Beneath them was my mobile phone. I hadn't risked trying to return it to my bag the night before. Now I realised I'd have to do so in broad daylight. But try as I might I couldn't find the phone. It wasn't under the life jacket I was sitting on, or – I realised with a rising sense of panic – the ones near it.

I had that feeling that always lands on me when I've lost something, anger that it's gone cut with annoying certainty that it can't have disappeared entirely: the phone had to be somewhere. I would have preferred it to be at the bottom of the sea rather than incriminatingly nearby. Was I misremembering where I'd put it? No! Perhaps I'd slept more restlessly than I realised and had dislodged it somehow, thrashing about.

That didn't stack up. I'd barely moved a muscle, because with my feet and hands bound I couldn't! And yet although I shifted all those life jackets about enough to make Amelia hiss, 'Whatever it is you're looking for, they're going to notice if you don't stop,' there was nothing beneath any of them, just the smooth white deck of the boat.

I glanced up when she said that, to check that Barrel-man was still looking the other way, and he was. But my relief was quickly snuffed out when I saw that Mo was indeed watching me. Our eyes locked.

For a second I was certain that he would alert the captain, or Barrel-man, because they'd made it plain that we were his responsibility: any fuss from us, and he'd be in the firing line too. But instead of calling out in alarm the boy just held my gaze for a moment, both palms raised, as if to say, 'It's OK, keep calm, I've got this.'

Infuriating!

17.

Breakfast that morning was the same as dinner the night before, only this time I ate it. I'd made my point. The flatbread tasted of salted butter and the jerky was infused with some sort of chorizo-like spice. Washed down with more lemonade, it was actually pretty good. But Xander, hunched beside me, didn't seem to want his.

'I don't feel too good,' he explained when I asked why.

'What sort of not-good?' asked Amelia.

'Swimming head, lurching stomach. But it's just the swell,' he said. 'I've had seasickness before.'

I'd not really noticed, but now that he pointed it out, I saw the sea had got up. Except for a few ripples it had been flat as a lake since we set out the day before, but now we were lifting and falling, tugged on by the cruiser over black-green humps.

They were coming at us from an angle, causing *Thunderbolt* to pitch and roll at the same time. We were making uneven and lurching progress beneath a grey sky that

I now saw was stacked with purplish clouds. That morning they boiled up to blot out the morning sun.

The weather went bad quickly. Stiff wind soon built to a proper gale which knocked whitecaps off the waves, whipping up spray which combined with the spume gouged by the plunging bow to fill the rushing air. We were wet through before the rain began.

Xander fought the seasickness, but couldn't beat it, and eventually had to drag himself up in the stern so that he could be violently sick over the transom between the big outboards. I felt for him. So did Mo. He cut the tape binding Xander's ankles so he could at least brace himself against the bucking of the boat.

With Xander throwing up over the stern, Amelia tapped Mo on the shoulder and said, 'Cinnarizine, cyclizine, promethazine, are all types of . . .'

'Antihistamine.'

'Used to counter?'

'Motion sickness, among other things.'

'If you pass me my dry-bag, I've got a packet I can open for Xander.'

'You brought them, but you're not sick yourself.'

'Better safe than sorry.'

At Amelia's direction, Mo retrieved her bag from the bulkhead. She spent long enough rooting around in it to make me think she was up to something, but in fact she did have some pills buried among her stuff, and she did give Xander a couple. He washed them down with water, but frankly they didn't stay on board long: he was in a right state.

Before the storm proper hit us the captain appeared at the rail again and gave the order to transfer us to the bigger vessel. Only Barrel-man, still lounging in Pete's chair and looking about as bothered by the weather as a rock might, was to remain behind.

One by one Mo freed us of our bindings and led us forward, up onto the prow, to make the jump across to the platform off the cruiser's stern. I went last. Although the tape around my ankles hadn't bothered me too badly, now that it was undone my legs were weirdly stiff. I felt unsteady on my feet, and it wasn't just the fault of the waves.

The others were suffering too. I'd seen Mo take an incapacitated Xander by the hand and tell him when to jump, and I'd also seen Amelia lose her footing climbing up onto the prow. She had to clutch the boy for support. I was damn well going to make the trip without help. But though I have a pretty good sense of balance, it's one thing to sit in a bucking boat, another to stand up, and harder still to walk when your legs have gone to sleep.

Mo, who hadn't spent an age tied up, and who apparently lived on a boat anyway, understandably made the whole thing look like nothing at all. But although I did my best to concentrate and ignore the numbness of dead-wood calves, I mistimed my jump, leaping as the prow rose and the platform dropped away. This turned what would have been a three-foot drop into a ten-foot one. I landed with an awful thump and crumpled to my knees.

Mo caught me round the shoulders and asked, 'You're OK, you're not hurt?'

'I'm fine,' I growled, standing up.

'Good, come then,' he said, and having slackened off the tow line to put a good thirty metres between us and the dive boat, he ushered me up the rusty ladder, across the cruiser's rear deck, and into the cabin itself.

From the speedboat I'd not worked out the size of this enclosed space. It dropped away from the captain's seat in the wheelhouse – he barely looked at me as I passed by – down a set of steep stairs, and opened up into a cramped room lined with benches bolted to the floor, between which stood a table, similarly secured.

Visible beyond this room was a further, hutch-like space extending into the prow of the boat. I made out a figure – one of the two gunmen I'd seen yesterday, presumably – lying on some sort of cot. His outstretched foot was stuck in a flip-flop that seemed to have been made from an offcut of old tyre.

The last member of the five-man pirate crew – or, more properly, four men and a boy – was up on the jump seat in the wheelhouse next to the captain, looking down at us through the open cabin door, cradling a gun in his lap like a little dog.

Presumably they shifted us into this enclosed cabin to shelter us from the worst of the weather, but to be honest I'd have preferred to stay on Pete's boat. This one stank of rotten fish drenched in cat pee and cloaked in diesel fumes. Never mind the rolling of the boat, the smell was enough to make me want to throw up.

Poor Xander had nothing much left to get rid of, but

immediately looked like he was going to be sick again, so Mo pulled open a cupboard door to reveal a tiny toilet cubicle. There was barely space in there for Xander to lean over, but that's what he did, retching into the bowl while the cupboard door swung open and shut, hiding and revealing him, until he managed to grab the inner handle and hold it shut.

It hit me again then: we should have been eating fruit salad and waffles in beautiful Ras Nungwi, safe from the storm, getting ready to return to England, but instead we were stuck here being thrown around by the waves in this stinking pirate boat, heading god-knew-where, hungry and wet, one of us sick, at the mercy of armed maniacs, our only hope this strange Mo kid. Pete was lost at sea. Mum would be beside herself. And it was all my fault. I wanted to punch something out of frustration.

'Do you think this boat is safer than Pete's then?' Amelia asked. She was trying to sound conversational but for her to have asked me, no expert in boats, such a non-scientific question, I knew she had to be out of her mind with worry.

My reply, 'It's as safe as any other,' sounded so lame I felt I had to add something better to reassure her. 'Though these guys are crooks, I'll bet they know exactly what they're doing when it comes to negotiating a storm at sea. And anyway, none of them seem bothered.'

Nobody asked his opinion but Mo said, 'The captain, he is very experienced, it's true,' and coming from him that seemed a solid enough observation to raise a nod from Amelia.

Xander emerged unsteadily. I helped him back to one of the benches. All the blood seemed to have drained from his

88

face. Being half Nigerian he is normally a healthy brown, but he was sludge-grey now. He lay out flat at my suggestion, but it was impossible for him to rest as he had to keep reaching out and bracing himself. I tried to help him by wedging myself between his legs and the table, keeping him in place.

The boat had begun to buck and dive even more ferociously, and every now and then a wave hit us hard enough to make me think the hull would split open like a pea pod hit with a hammer, spilling us into the depths. The thump of those waves was nothing compared to the noise of the rain, however. It sounded like a million marbles slamming into the deck, the wheelhouse roof and the exposed stern, a torrent pouring from the sky with such venom that if a wave didn't split our hull the rain would surely fill the boat and sink us.

I'd tried to reassure Amelia, but I was fighting back my own panic. As the storm swelled around us I'd never felt smaller, more vulnerable, more sure I was about to die.

18.

I hung on to one thought: if the boat didn't sink the storm would eventually pass. I couldn't have told you whether we were tossed about for six hours or twenty-six. The boat pitched and slammed and wallowed and lurched endlessly. It was too much to take in, so I sort of switched off, blotting everything out.

Though it had built quickly, the storm fizzled out very gradually indeed. I didn't feel it fade, just began to notice other things. For example, I realised the guy in the bunk room was listening to something, a voice coming from somewhere, perhaps a shortwave radio? It was all static and gibberish for the most part, but I swear I heard a repeated 'mayday' at one point. A little later he lumbered past us and up the stairs to the wheelhouse to talk to the captain. I don't know what he said but he sounded animated, and shortly afterwards the pitch of our engines deepened.

I also noticed that an inch or so of water had flooded the floor. As we rocked, it swept from side to side picking up bits of plastic wrapper, twine, bottle tops, and the like. The water must have come down the stairs. We'd have known about it if we'd sprung an actual leak, surely?

Amelia seemed to read my mind. She pointed at the floor and said, 'Is that a problem?' I have to admit I was relieved when Mo shook his head. At first that little lake sloshed about all over the place. In time it rolled from side to side more slowly. The rattle of the rain became a hiss which gradually quietened to nothing. In the quiet the cabin seemed bigger and brighter. The stairs lit up. I've no idea if we'd actually sailed right through a full day of storm and into the following morning, but the sky was now weakly bright again overhead.

Xander woke up, raised himself on one arm, and said, 'Mo, can you ask permission for us to go up on deck?'

Mo looked nervous. 'Why?' he said.

'I need some air.'

Amelia chipped in: 'You'll need some water too. We all do. But you must be properly dehydrated.'

'I have a splitting headache.'

'That'll be why.'

Mo nodded. 'I'll see what I can do,' he said.

From my vantage point to one side of the stairs I watched Mo as he talked to the captain. I couldn't hear the captain's response but knew it was positive from the boy's super-grateful nodding. In my opinion, he really needed to grow a backbone. All the same, it was a huge relief to be allowed up those stairs again. The breeze on my face was enough to make me feel almost human again.

Mo ushered us to the stern and told us to sit down there. The first thing I noticed was that Pete's speedboat had disappeared. The rope that once attached it to us was coiled neatly on the platform below. Neither Barrel-man nor the gunman with the tyre-tread flip-flops were aboard with us, so they'd presumably gone off in the dive launch together somewhere. That angered me: it made the fact that they'd stolen the boat all the more obvious, I suppose.

Mo disappeared again. When he surfaced, he had more of the same food, but the plastic bottle he brought turned out to contain actual water this time.

'I've never understood why it's called finding your sea legs,' said Amelia.

'It's a balance thing,' I said.

'I know, but surely finding your sea stomach is more important.'

I'd thought it was morning, but from the position of the sun in the sky, low among tumbled clouds, it had to be afternoon. Though I'd lost track of time, something didn't feel right about that. It took me a while to realise I was right: the sun was gaining height, not losing it, meaning it was indeed morning and we were headed south-west rather than north-east.

'Why the change of course?' I asked aloud, resenting the fact that only Mo could answer the question.

'I think perhaps they heard something on the radio, and are investigating,' he said.

'What do you mean, investigating?'

The answer became clear soon enough. We'd not been

up on deck long before a notch appeared on the horizon, dead ahead. We were making our way steadily straight for whatever it was. The thing split in two as we approached. Pete's idling speedboat was one half of the equation, the other was a becalmed yacht with a broken mast.

It was lying low in the water, clearly half flooded. I put two and two together to work out what Mo had been reluctant to say. Most likely the mayday call I'd overheard during the storm had come from this stricken boat. The pirate captain had dispatched his new quick launch to find it.

I knew before I saw the yacht's owners – a white-haired man and a younger woman with sunburnt shoulders, who were taped back to back next to the shattered mast – that the pirates hadn't sped here to offer assistance. They were stealing anything of value. Flip-flops was minding Pete's boat, but Barrel-man, the assault rifle slung across his back, exited from the half-submerged interior of the yacht carrying something and dropped it into the open mouth of a kitbag on deck.

'What's happening?' asked Amelia.

'They're robbing those people,' muttered Xander.

'That boat looks like it's sinking though,' said Amelia. 'They'll bring that couple aboard, right?'

Mo looked away.

'They won't leave them on a sinking boat, surely.'

Mo didn't reply.

Both the captain and the remaining guard on our boat were fixated by what was going on with the yacht. That meant they had their backs turned. I cast around for anything

I might use as a weapon, but there was nothing. Hitting one of them over the head with a half empty water bottle wouldn't achieve anything.

Even if we managed to take control of this boat, we'd never outrun Pete's launch with Barrel-man at the helm. A length of thin plastic cord, coiled in the bilge, was the only object of any possible use within reach, so I picked it up and wrapped it round my hips, then concealed it below the waistband of my shorts. It might come in handy for tying something to something, possibly.

The poor couple on the boat were keeping their eyes down. I noticed that the man had a livid gash running the length of his left shin. He was bleeding onto the deck. Surely they'd have a first aid kit on board?

I was about to ask Mo to suggest Barrel-man look for it, when I spotted the speck of another boat on the horizon. It was coming our way. If I was right and the yacht had put out a distress call during the storm it would make sense that other boats in the area might respond to it as well.

The captain had also clocked this new inbound boat. He yelled something across the water, alerting Barrel-man and Flip-flops. Barrel-man dived into the half-submerged yacht again to retrieve another bag filled with I've no idea what, flung it and the other spoils across to Flip-flops in the speedboat, and followed himself, deftly jumping the gap. At the captain's order the two men began to ready the dive boat.

'We should do something,' I said.

'Like what?' replied Xander.

'Something to alert that boat. They're sailing into a trap.'

Mo grabbed my arm. 'Don't!' he hissed.

I might not have done what I did next if he hadn't been so insistent, but I wasn't about to take orders from Mo. I shook the boy off easily enough. Then I pulled my T-shirt over my head and waved it frantically in the air, a flag of distress.

It was a ludicrously weak attempt at a warning; unless somebody on the other boat had a pair of binoculars trained on me they'd never see me at that distance, but so what?

Xander hissed, 'That looks like a distress signal! It's as likely to make them think we need help and draw them to us as it is to warn them off!'

Like an idiot I ignored him, and regretted it almost instantly. The approaching boat may still have been too far away to spot me but the big bear-like guard who'd stayed on the cabin cruiser with the captain, the one who cradled his assault rifle with such tenderness, saw what I was doing. He moved very quickly for such a big guy. In three or four steps he was slap bang in front of me with the gun pointed at my midriff and a look about as blank as that sand tiger shark's in his eye.

19.

Somebody shrieked, 'No, no, no!' beside me. I thought it was Amelia, or possibly Xander, but it turned out to be Mo. With hindsight that's pretty scary: Mo knew these guys and definitely thought the big guard might pull the trigger. But that wasn't his plan. Although he advanced pointing the gun's muzzle at me he swung the butt forward as he arrived and slammed it straight into my solar plexus.

The blow drove the air from my lungs and knocked me flat on my back.

I've been winded before, but this was different. The nearest thing I can liken it to is the time, aged eight, I accidentally gave myself an electric shock trying to get a burning bagel out of the toaster with a fork. The electricity shooting through me then felt like icy lightning. It bounced me across the kitchen. I cracked my head open on the corner of the island unit.

Now, on my back in the bilge, trying to draw a breath was impossible. The air had somehow turned to tarmac.

I had to cough up lumps of the stuff before I could catch a lungful of actual sea breeze.

He didn't hit me again, and mercifully he didn't hit any of the others either. He didn't need to: the blow to me made a good enough point. By the time I'd clawed my way upright onto one knee the guard wasn't even bothering to stand over me.

'You OK?' said Xander. Both he and Mo were helping me up.

I tried to say 'yes', but it came out more like a cough and tasted, faintly but worryingly, of blood.

Xander looked unconvinced.

Amelia, taking me at face value, said, 'Good, but possibly that was just a little bit pointless.'

'It was brave,' said Mo. At least he didn't follow up with 'but'.

Focusing on the horizon I saw that the approaching boat was a fair bit closer. It looked like some sort of deep-sea fishing outfit, prickling with stumpy rods. We'd be off Kenya here: the red dots aboard were no doubt game fishermen out of Mombasa or perhaps Watamu. What would the wealthy fishermen on board see? The battered cruiser we were on, a sleek speedboat, and a foundering, swamped yacht with a snapped mast.

No doubt they'd picked up the same distress call as Flip-flops. Would they wonder why nobody was now on the other end of the yacht's shortwave radio, or were they assuming that it had stopped working? Presumably they'd expect us, the rescuers, to have a working radio and the ability to speak to them. All the pirates were in view: none on a radio. Maybe that's what made the fishermen slow down when they were still a fair way off, or perhaps they caught sight of the two sailors bound either side of the broken mast-stump. It certainly wasn't my flag-T-shirt waving that made them alter course. But they'd got wind that something was wrong, and by the time I was able to breathe properly again – despite the molten pain in my chest – their boat was veering away.

Immediately the dive boat gave chase. Pete had always run it up to top speed gradually, but Barrel-man must have thrown both throttles all the way forward at once. The boat pretty much leaped from the sea. It careened off a low wave and the propellers bit nothing before slamming into the water again.

The captain slewed us round too, headed towards the fishing boat at a comparatively leisurely pace. This meant we were leaving the sailors on their swamped yacht.

I couldn't stop myself looking back as we moved off. To begin with they just sat there, but after a few moments, when we'd opened up a safe distance, I was relieved to see movement.

The sunburnt woman, evidently having managed to tear herself free of the gaffer tape, got up and went to liberate her partner. His head was still bowed. That cut on his leg must have been painful. And yet – I tried to conjure up some hope for them – their yacht hadn't sunk any lower in the water while we'd been alongside. Hopefully their distress signal was still pulsing, or the radio was still operational, or they had flares. I grasped at these straws as they slipped from sight.

Without Pete's boat in pursuit I'm pretty sure the deep-sea fishermen would have made their escape. But the speedboat, a greyhound after a cat, ran them down in a matter of minutes. We floundered along, following the chase. I saw something flashing in the dive boat well before I heard the staccato crackling of gunfire.

The anglers had come to a halt by the time we caught up, with the dive boat slowly circling them. Would they have their own weapons with which to fight back? It didn't seem so, or at least if they were armed they must have thought themselves outgunned, and since they couldn't flee or fight they'd opted instead to give in. The speedboat burbled back to us and the big guard from our boat jumped in. The pirates evidently wanted a two-man boarding party for this catch.

My first thought then was that the captain was the sole pirate left on board with us. He must have reckoned Mo would still be watching his back – and perhaps the boy was – but something about the way he had tried to stop me getting myself shot made me doubt it.

'Guys,' I said.

'What are you thinking?' asked Xander.

The burning in my chest meant I felt completely unready to follow through with what I was about to propose, which may have been why I said, 'Isn't it obvious?' instead of spelling it out.

Mo said, 'No! You must learn! It is madness to resist now.'

At which Amelia said, 'Completely. Say we throw the guy overboard. Then what? Off we set in a slow boat to nowhere. You think the armed crew in that power boat will simply wave us off?'

Through gritted teeth I said, 'We have to do something though.'

'Yes,' murmured Mo. 'But only when we can be effective. We should wait. I will help you plot a proper escape, once we reach land.'

Since we'd been captured, I'd not thought about when we would set foot ashore again. I'd not allowed myself to dwell on the question because I'd actually been more worried about 'if' than 'when'.

But unless these pirates were planning on throwing us overboard – which made no sense given they'd kept us safe till now – they would presumably have to hang on to us until they made landfall.

Operating out of a forty-foot boat, they wouldn't be staying out at sea indefinitely. Sooner or later they would have to dock to cash in their loot and pick up supplies.

Mo was right; the thing to do was wait until then. But watching Barrel-man, Flip-flops and the Bear, who'd socked me with his rifle, as they prepared to board the fishing boat, I felt sick that I could do nothing to help now.

20.

It turned out that the deep-sea fishermen hadn't in fact reached the same conclusion as me. The three guys on deck with their hands in the air did make it look like they'd surrendered, but as Barrel-man brought the dive boat alongside so the guards could climb aboard, a fourth fisherman jumped up among the stumpy rods sticking from the fishing boat's stern.

He had a pistol in his hand. It bucked three times in quick succession, then jammed.

The dive boat was close by. This fisherman had waited to take his chance at close range. And he hit his mark. The Bear who'd battered me immediately spun sideways and dropped to his knee among the life jackets still spread out in the hold. But he'd barely thumped to the deck before the other guard, Flip-flops, unleashed his semi-automatic.

Compared to the *pock-pock-pock* of the pistol, Flip-flops' gun was shatteringly loud. He let loose in bursts. Chunks of fibreglass sprayed from the deck of the fishing launch and the man who'd fired the pistol was thrown clear out of sight.

The Bear was already clawing himself up out of the bilge. His left arm was vivid with blood from the elbow down. With his other hand he thrust his gun towards Barrel-man, who took it. They were swapping roles.

The Bear took control of the dive launch one-handed, Barrel-man covered the target boat with the rifle, and Flip-flops scrambled across the rail as the two boats came together. Once he was safely aboard Barrel-man followed, and then the Bear drew Pete's boat away. Either the guy was in shock or just incredibly tough. He inspected his hurt arm with mild interest, as if it belonged to somebody else, before picking Pete's chamois leather out of the compartment next to the driver's seat and wrapping it tightly around the wound.

I couldn't see what was happening on board the fishing boat, but somebody started shouting. The sound was immediately drowned out by another crackle of gunfire. There was a high scream, then sobbing.

'They've killed him,' Amelia stated.

She was right. Barrel-man levered the limp body of one of the anglers – presumably the guy who'd tried to fight back – up over the gunwale. He'd been shot in the head. I tried not to take in what was left of his face, just registered a middle-aged white guy with thick limbs and a big stomach. His T-shirt rose up to reveal its paleness as Barrel-man slid him over the side of the boat.

This seemed to be the pirates' method: show everyone you mean business by making an example of at least one victim. In retrospect Pete had been lucky to be thrown overboard alive. Lucky or extremely unlucky, depending on how you looked at it, I thought grimly.

The body rolled over a couple of feet beneath the surface, blood clouding the clear blue water. I didn't want to stare at the dead man but couldn't help it. He was drifting our way. I tried to focus on the poor guys still aboard the fishing boat. One of them was shaking so hard it was visible from this distance. I couldn't see either pirate aboard, but presumably one of them had his gun trained on the guys on deck, while the other was doing the looting.

'What was that?' Xander asked nobody in particular. He was pointing at the water right where the dead guy was floating. A dark blur rocketed up into the corpse, punching it through the surface, before immediately dragging it down again. The first shark still had hold of the man's leg when the second one struck his body, and a third veered in on the second one's tail. More immediately joined the fray. The water was soon boiling with them, their thrashing enough to create pink foam. It was a chilling sight, and if I had struggled to look away beforehand I was mesmerised now. Amelia and Xander were too. Only Mo kept his eyes on the fishing boat.

'That happened so fast,' said Xander.

'It's a common misconception that sharks can smell blood from miles away,' said Amelia quietly. 'Their sense of smell is acute, but it's actually more like a few hundred metres. These ones will have been in the area already. Maybe they were following the fishing boat.'

'Or us,' I muttered.

'Less likely,' said Amelia decisively.

It didn't take long for the frenzy to die down. The sharks quickly dragged what was left of the body too deep to see. As far as I could remember Pete hadn't been bleeding when Barrel-man threw him overboard. He'd been conscious, he was strong, he was a formidable swimmer, with a life jacket, and a good knowledge of the currents, and . . . the more I tried to convince myself the dive master might have survived, the heavier the dread lay in the pit of my stomach.

Barrel-man was in view again now, ordering the anglers to hand over watches, wallets, phones. They gave up everything immediately, no doubt wanting the pirates gone as quickly as possible. Flip-flops passed two bags full of spoils they'd rinsed from the fishermen across to the one-armed Bear in the stern of the dive boat, and within minutes we were pulling away from the fishermen entirely. Though not as forlorn as the yacht before it, the fishing boat seemed equally adrift. Had the pirates incapacitated it, or would they be able to make their way back to the safety of port? I asked Mo.

He shrugged. 'Sometimes the engine is broken in the aftermath.'

'Nice use of the passive tense,' said Amelia.

I wasn't sure exactly what she meant by that but got the gist: these guys tended to maroon their victims at sea. 'Where are we headed now?' I asked Mo.

He gave another shrug. 'I don't know, but I'll listen out.'

'Not back to port ourselves then?'

'That depends,' he said, but didn't elaborate.

Having realised we'd be returning to land at some point,

it struck me now that I should do whatever I could to make it happen sooner rather than later. But what? Pretending to fall ill wouldn't work. We weren't that valuable to them. What they cared about was their ability to hunt down boats. How could I make it harder for them to do that?

'Mo,' I said. 'Do you think you can persuade the boss to put me back in Pete's boat?'

'I doubt it,' Mo replied.

'Tell him we'd be less likely to mutiny if we were separated,' said Xander. 'Divide and conquer, et cetera.'

'That's not quite what it means,' said Amelia, 'But still. Why do you want to be stuck back there with those monsters anyway?' she added, flicking a thumb at Barrel-man, Flip-flops and the Bear, puttering along behind us.

'I just do. Trust me.'

'I'll ask,' said Mo. 'But don't hold your breath.'

'I've never understood that expression,' Amelia said, with her does-not-actually-compute face on. It was a relief to see it – familiar and reassuring – again, given the contrast with what we'd just witnessed. 'When I ask a question, I never hold my breath while waiting for the answer.'

Mo looked like he might reply but he must have sensed my agitation, because instead of debating the point he set off to put the actual question to the captain.

21.

Mo had underestimated his influence over the captain who, it turned out, thought reorganising us all across the two boats was a good precaution. Xander did well to come up with that idea. Maybe my T-shirt-waving helped. I was the troublemaker to be kept apart from the others.

Barrel-man, who seemed to be second in command, would watch me in the speedboat. Mo joined us as an extra pair of eyes. Flip-flops and the captain rode in the bigger boat with Xander, Amelia and the wounded Bear, who retreated to his bunk, as if a quick lie-down might cure him of the bullet he'd taken to the forearm.

It's possible the captain would have set sail for home to patch up his man, injured in the attack, but I couldn't be sure of that. With the speedboat out of action, however, they'd be less capable of hunting down more victims. Helping Pete prepare to launch the boat earlier in the week had given me an idea of how I could successfully sabotage it, but I had to wait for nightfall before I could risk executing my plan.

I spent the time on the rearmost bench seat, looking out at our wake. Once again, the pirates had chosen to tow the speedboat at a safe distance behind the cruiser, so for now the big outboards were silent. In the aftermath of the storm the sea had turned glassy and we were drawn on smoothly, tugged by the cruiser, our wake quietly etched across the mirrored face of the sea. I ran my eyes out to where the expanding silver V disappeared over and over again. As the afternoon dropped into evening the wake vanished closer to the boat. After nightfall I had to look straight down to see it.

At some point Mo had come to sit closer to me. I could tell that he wanted to talk to me, but the feeling wasn't mutual. I still didn't know whether I could trust him. It seemed so, but why take the risk?

Well, with his help I could have made sure Barrel-man didn't wake up and spot me when I set to work; without it I'd have to wait until I was sure both of them were sound asleep before taking the plunge. Possibly because I knew that Mo would try to persuade me not to do it, I decided on the latter course of action.

I lay back on the bench seat and waited for Barrel-man's head to loll and stay lolled. He was still sprawling in Pete's chair with his feet up on the boat's dash. When Mo got no joy out of me he retreated to his own bench so that he could lie down flat. I watched him too, waiting until both of them had stayed still for a good quarter of an hour before chancing it.

My plan, such as it was, was to use Pete's siphon to do

107

exactly what he'd warned me to avoid doing with it at all costs. I'd made sure I was stationed in the stern, next to the fuel tank and within reach of the compartment in which I knew Pete had stowed the long, thin coil of fuel hose we'd used as a siphon.

When the time came, I pried open that compartment super-slowly and retrieved it. Then I sprang the catch on the dive boat's fuel tank. So far, so good. I unwound the coiled pipe. This was the moment of truth. Would it be long enough, fully uncoiled, for one end, draped between the big outboards, to reach into the sea, while the other end was tucked inside the fuel tank?

Easily, it turned out. To make sure I got a good flow going I sucked on the other end of the hose hard and long enough to flood my mouth with saltwater. It didn't taste as bad as all that. Once the water started to flow, I carefully angled the end of the hose I'd sucked into the fuel tank.

Sitting where I was, so close to the tank, the wash of the sea against the hull wasn't quite loud enough to mask the tinkling of seawater into the petrol, and though that probably wouldn't have been the case even just a few feet away, I couldn't be sure, so it was a relief when I found I could stop the trickling sound by angling the tip of the tube sideways into the lip of the tank.

Pete had explained that the engine could handle a bit of water contamination, but a lot would quickly wreck the injectors, so I topped the tank up a fair way, not right to the top, because that would have made the tampering obvious, but with enough seawater to cause a problem.

I kept one eye on the man in the captain's chair, occasionally checking that Mo was still asleep on his side. It's amazing that a bit of suction can make water flow uphill. Amelia would probably have wanted to explain the physics of the thing – no doubt Mo could recite whatever equations made it happen too – but for me the incapacitating sound of the trickling was enough.

When I was sure I'd trashed the fuel properly I eased the tube out of the tank and gently secured the lid again. The whole operation, carried out so slowly, had taken a good ten minutes, and I wasn't done yet. Not quite. Inevitably, it was with the last bit of the job – returning the length of hose to its rightful place – that I messed up.

22.

I must have coiled the hose too tight. As I'd pulled it up over the stern, I wound it round one hand with the other, hoping that by keeping it in a ball I'd stop it slapping about. Water dripped in my lap as I did this, but silently, so it didn't matter. Once I had the coil ready, I eased open the storage compartment beneath my seat and gently pushed the bundle inside.

Maybe I pressed it down too low, in among the other stuff, close to the hinge, or possibly it was just that winding the hose up tight gave the thing a spring-like purpose: to unravel. Either way, when I let go the compartment door sprung open immediately and a half empty plastic oil canister flopped out of the door and down onto the fibreglass deck.

I grabbed at it and missed, knocking it sideways against the hull. The hollow clattering sound it made was very different to the gentle plashing of the water around us and, as I was stuffing the damn thing back in the compartment, out of the corner of my eye I saw Barrel-man jerk upright in his seat.

He was shrugging himself awake and began to turn around.

If he'd done so he'd have seen that I was awake and panic-rummaging.

But a much louder wallop distracted him.

It shocked me too. I felt the noise as well as heard it, and briefly wondered whether we'd struck something in the water. But the noise was in fact Mo hitting the actual deck. He'd rolled off the bench. Now he was groggily sitting up.

Barrel-man fixed on him.

Mo, still rubbing his head, murmured something apologetic.

At that Barrel-man swung around in his chair and lifted his feet up next to the steering wheel again.

Had the noise of the stupid canister rolling on the deck disturbed Mo as well as the psychotic pirate? Possibly. Amelia would have come out with something about probability, decibel levels and heightened states of awareness, I imagine, but I preferred to trust my gut.

It told me the boy had fallen off his bench deliberately, to create a distraction. As in, to help me. That would mean that he'd seen what I was up to and not done anything to make me stop. He'd just covered for me when it looked like Barrel-man might rumble my act of sabotage.

The trouble with having a reliable gut instinct is that you learn over time it's foolish to ignore it. If Mo really was meaning to help me – us – that was a good thing. Why did it niggle me then? Possibly it was the thought that he'd want something in return that set me on edge. I was in his debt now, and I didn't particularly like it. That said, I'd have liked it a lot less if the maniac in Pete's chair had caught me.

Over the next few minutes I eased my way along the bench seat until I was abreast of Mo, close enough to whisper, 'That was no accident.'

'Go back to sleep,' he said.

'I wasn't asleep and neither were you.'

'Whatever. Sleep now.'

'You're not denying it then.'

'Nobody has to deny anything,' he whispered, before repeating, 'Go back to sleep.'

'What do you want from me?' I muttered under my breath.

'Eh?' He sounded genuinely incredulous.

'Why cover for me if you don't want something in return?'

'Surely you see,' he said at length, 'that I want exactly the same thing as you. I'm literally in the same boat. Just because they stole me from my village in Somalia, not from some luxury holiday resort, doesn't mean I don't want to escape from these people every bit as much as you do. The only difference is that I've wanted to for longer, and I know them much better than you, which maybe makes me more cautious. But if I can see the point in a plan and think you can get away with it, why wouldn't I want to help?'

Surely it was better to admit the truth of what he was saying and take him on as an ally. It wasn't as if I had lots of other avenues of hope.

'You want further proof?' he went on. 'Your mobile phone. Where is it?'

The truth was, I'd forgotten I didn't know. After I used

112

it to contact Mum, I'd fallen asleep with it beneath me and woken to find it gone. Then in the upheaval of the storm and everything since I'd not thought of it.

'I saw you fetch it from your bag, use it, and fail to hide it properly.'

'I hid it beneath the life jackets.'

'You dislodged it while you slept. When I woke up, before you, it was in plain view on the bottom of the boat.'

'Where the hell is it now then?'

'Your phone is back where it was before you took the risk of using it. Much less hazardous for me to be seen looking through your stuff than it would have been if they'd spotted you returning it. They'll probably take it from you anyway. But for now, your phone is back in your bag, where I put it.'

23.

I took ages to drift off after Mo told me that. I'm not a great believer in the relevance of dreams – I mean, I've had some pretty stupid ones – but that night, when I did eventually sleep, it was only in bursts. I kept jerking awake from a dream in which the frayed end of a rope had slipped from my hand, dropping me into a vast emptiness. That horrible lurching sensation. Where would I land? Ugh.

I must have found deep sleep at some point, however, as I woke to the thin light of just-before-dawn. Opening one eye, I saw Mo fiddling about with something in the stern. What was that there, in full view, at his feet? Only one of Pete's empty fuel canisters. With weary deliberation he picked the can up, looked over his shoulder at Barrel-man, who was still asleep in his chair, and plonked the thing down again loudly. Then he screwed the cap tight, or pretended to at least.

I was about to protest when he repeated the operation. Barrel-man hadn't woken at the first 'plonk', but he did now.

Far from trying to cover anything up, Mo made it perfectly obvious that he'd just filled up the tank, securing the fuel cap and tightening the lid of the canister and returning it to where I'd stored it – along with the other one, both of them completely empty – in the forward compartment.

Barrel-man looked on idly, one hand under his T-shirt, scratching his washboard stomach. Bored and bleary, the pirate watched Mo stow the canister without comment, then hawked up a lump of phlegm and spat it overboard.

'What the hell were you doing?' I muttered when he came back to the boat's stern.

'I'd have thought that was obvious.'

It wasn't, not to me, and I didn't like that one bit.

Mo smiled. 'Don't worry,' he said. 'It's all part of the plan.'

'What plan?'

'Your plan!' he said, a you-really-don't-get-it? glint in his eye.

We were still tethered to the battered cruiser, which tugged us along gently. The water was silver this morning. We were headed north again. I tried to work out how far we would have travelled overnight. Twelve hours at what, eight or so miles an hour? About a hundred miles, give or take. Not knowing where we'd turned around meant I couldn't accurately predict how far up the coast we'd come. It was tempting to ask Mo if he knew, but I didn't. I was still trying to figure out what his messing about with the fuel canisters could have contributed to my sabotaging the dive boat.

I soon found out. Before the sun had risen high enough to turn the sea its rightful blue the cruiser slackened its pace ahead of us, the captain expertly bringing us alongside.

The pirates conferred. Their conversation sounded urgent. It turned out – Mo told me later – that Flip-flops had intercepted another radio message, this one from a nearby catamaran with a sick crew member. The captain thought there could be tasty pickings aboard. He wanted Barrel-man to give chase, and, with Flip-flops and his gun aboard, ordered us to get going.

Mo immediately untied the rope tethering us to the cruiser and Barrel-man hit the ignition. The outboards roared to life. I was surprised for a nanosecond, then realised that there would of course have been clean fuel in the pipe connecting them to the fuel tank.

Once they'd sucked in a shot of my gas-and-seawater cocktail the engines started coughing hard enough to make the fibreglass hull shiver. That shivering quickly became the death rattle of a soon-to-be corpse, before both engines cut out completely.

The boat hadn't made it more than a couple of hundred yards. The captain in his cruiser quickly caught up with us again. It turned out that the wounded Bear was the team's best mechanic. He was hampered by the sling supporting his injured arm, but soon worked out what was wrong, and within minutes he and Barrel-man were examining the canister Mo had – apparently openly – tipped into the boat's fuel tank.

Interrogating the boy, Barrel-man's voice had a menacing edge to it. Mo, palms up, was the picture of innocence. 'I was just trying to be helpful!' his pleading eyes said. He sniffed at the empty fuel can himself and spoke insistently.

116

I could tell he was pointing out that the canister smelled strongly of petrol. And it did. There was probably still a dribble of the stuff in the bottom.

Barrel-man couldn't dispute the smell, but that didn't mean much: something must have been wrong with whatever Mo had added to the fuel tank. He looked angry enough to toss Mo overboard. But the Bear, more perplexed than cross, was perhaps secretly pleased to have to cut the trip short. From the sweat on his brow and the way he was gritting his teeth I could tell his arm was hurting more than his tough-guy status would let him admit.

He said something to Mo that made the boy scuttle off to re-tether us to the cruiser, and gave Barrel-man an it-can-be-fixed-but-not-here shrug.

If it was a mistake to smile in that moment, the bigger one was to let Barrel-man see. He's the sort of person whose anger doesn't fade. He needs to let it out.

I don't think he thought I was responsible for the fuel contamination. As far as he was concerned, Mo had been the one to add spoiled fuel to the mix, not me.

But he didn't like the look of me in that moment, and he didn't give me the chance to wipe the grin off my face myself. He did it for me himself. He closed the gap between us in two quick steps and hit me across the cheek and temple with a lightning-quick open palm.

It was as if a firework had gone off right next to my ear. I reeled sideways, my head ringing. He was jabbering at me furiously. I couldn't have made sense of English in that moment, much less Somali. The ringing in my ears was jet-engine loud. I thought he'd burst my eardrum.

I kept a malevolent eye on the pirate all morning, thinking it had been worth it. The bastard could slap me all he liked: it wouldn't bring the outboards back to life.

24.

A slice of coastline came into view while we were eating our lunch, which today was a single hardboiled egg. The yolk of mine was edged the exact same pale grey colour as the distant sliver of whichever country it was – Kenya or Somalia, I presumed – seen through the haze.

We made for the land mass obliquely as the afternoon wore on. Its contours darkened. By about four o'clock we were close enough to see the detail of the coastline, bays and headlands and stretches of scrub and sand, an occasional village, even the fringes of trees.

Seeing the palm trees made me think of Mum back on Zanzibar. I prayed her tough streak would see her through this ordeal. Like me, Mum's idea of a nightmare is being powerless. If there's a problem, she has to sort it. The odds don't matter. She's tenacious. That's why she's such an effective activist. But what, realistically, could she be doing to help us now? Unable to do anything, the worry would be eating her alive.

For some reason I assumed we would hold off landing until nightfall, that the pirates would want to return under the cover of darkness, spiriting us away without risk of detection. But I was wrong. Late in the afternoon with the sun still a good hour or two above the horizon, we veered landward and sailed straight into a scabby little harbour backed by a mess of corrugated sheds, with both boats in plain view.

The captain pulled the cruiser up to the ramshackle pontoon – made out of concrete and piled-up packing crates – next to a decent-sized boat that smelled of rotting fish. Nobody aboard it seemed to mind, and the pirates were instantly embroiled in a loud and cheerful conversation with a man on deck who paused in what he was doing – mending some sort of winch, it looked like – to shout equally happily back at him. At one point the captain went as far as to pull Amelia and Xander from the cabin so he could show them off to his friend. He also jerked his thumb at me, laughing.

A group of men gathered on the dock to look at Pete's boat, which Mo had skipped ashore to tie up. I have to hand it to him, he's good at knots. Barrel-man made it clear I should join him. I gathered our three dry-bags from the bulkhead, half thinking he'd scream at me to put them back, or worse still show me the palm of his hand uncomfortably quickly again, but he didn't seem to care. He was more interested in greeting the men gathering on the quay, who seemed good friends with all the pirate crew.

The atmosphere felt a bit like I imagine it would when soldiers return from war. More men showed up as news of our arrival quickly spread. If everyone hadn't been so happy to see the captain, Barrel-man, the wounded Bear and Flip-flops, I'd have been worried: looked at one way the crowd seemed hyper enough to be dangerous, but the mood was in fact more festive than angry.

Though nobody laid a finger on us I was frightened that they might, and suddenly very aware that Amelia was the only girl in sight. Whether or not she'd clocked that too I don't know, but her face, bowed to the dusty dock, was pretty ashen.

Mo hovered close to us, to one side of me one minute and the other side of Amelia the next. It seemed he was doing his best to form a one-man wall around us. 'When we move off, stick close together, with me, yes,' he said.

Why he thought we might do anything other than that, I don't know. I'd already ruled out trying to make a run for it. There were too many eyes on us, and in any case which way would we go? No, there'd be a better opportunity sooner or later, and when it came I'd make sure we were ready for it.

'Keep your heads down, and stay close together,' I said to Xander and Amelia.

Instantly I wished I hadn't when she replied, 'Why repeat stuff Mo's already said?'

I understood; when Amelia is stressed, she finds it even harder than usual not to point out things like repetition, superstition or lapses of logic. 'Nice to be back on dry land anyway,' I said in a lame attempt to calm her.

'Lovely,' said Xander.

'I'd hardly call it that,' said Amelia.

Ignoring this literal take on his sarcasm, Xander asked Mo what he thought would happen next.

'They'll take us to a safe house for the night, I expect,' he answered, adding, 'Don't worry, nothing's changed. You're still very valuable to them.'

The words 'safe' and 'valuable' were comforting, I suppose. We had little choice but to hope they were true.

Leaving the boats in the hands of the men who had gathered to greet them – one of whom was already at work bleeding the contaminated fuel from the dive boat's outboards – the pirates steered us away from the quay and into the little town behind it.

The sun was in our faces. It made the moving figures ahead of us silhouettes. A dog missing one of its front legs hopped out of our way, disappearing behind a half-built wall.

We moved in among the buildings. I tried to take it all in. One thing was for sure, this place was poor. We're not talking mud huts with grass roofs, but all the buildings were basic, a hotch-potch of breeze blocks and corrugated metal overlain in places with bits of plastic tarpaulin.

That wall there was braced with three logs; one end of each was jammed in the ground with the other angled up towards the roofline. The wall itself still looked like it was about to fall over. It would kill that chicken pecking at its base if it did.

The street was unpaved; dust rose around us as we moved forward. A filthy white car stood in the lee of the next building we passed. It had no windscreen.

The first children I'd seen, younger than us by far, were

playing on a bit of scrub near where we turned left. They were using a plastic bottle as a football, kicking it about without much enthusiasm.

Spotting us, they stopped to watch us pass. One of the littlest broke from the group and ran in among our legs, hand outstretched, asking for something.

I've no idea what he was after, but I do know what he got: a cuff round the head from Barrel-man not much softer than the one he'd given me on the boat. The kid can't have been more than four but instead of squealing or bursting into tears he just ran away laughing.

Though we'd only ventured inland a few hundred metres, the heat had already intensified, prickly and dry. Sweat ran down my face. I tried to keep track of the route we'd taken. As we rounded the next corner, still at the centre of an excited throng, one building stood out. It was painted that intense blue colour you see on Greek islands. A woman in a brilliant orange headscarf leaned in its doorway. Her face, framed by the scarf, was completely set; I stared at it until we were marched out of sight and didn't see it flicker, much less move.

Xander had noticed her too. 'Nice welcoming smile,' he muttered.

'We're not here as guests,' said Amelia.

'Fair point,' he replied. 'But still.'

Eventually we came to another beaten-up-looking building with a rusted metal door set in a low frame. I had to duck as we went through it. A guy with a squint so pronounced it almost made me overlook the AK-47 he had slung over his shoulder welcomed Flip-flops – and us – with a smile.

The clamour of voices in the street behind us dropped a notch after he clanged the door shut behind us, but didn't disappear entirely. At one remove, the chatter sounded celebratory.

What little light there was in the shack's front section took a moment to see by, and the inner room Flip-flops and Squint ushered us into beyond that hallway was darker still. I was still trying to figure out what – and who – was in it with us when I heard the metallic grinding of a bolt sliding shut.

A second lock clunked immediately after the first.

My eyes gradually adjusted to the gloom.

I made out two narrow beds pushed up against the walls of a room about half the size of mine back home. Either they were punishing Mo for his mistake with the fuel or they simply didn't trust him not to run away on land, for here he was, walled up with us.

We stood in silence a moment. I for one felt suddenly exhausted, and Amelia was swaying on her feet. Xander guided her to sit down, and seeing her take the weight off her feet made me want to do the same so badly I think I let out a groan.

'Four people, two beds,' said Mo. He looked from me to Xander and said, 'Jack was up most of the night. We can cope on the floor for now, yes?'

I sat down on the dusty concrete floor immediately, with my back pressed to the bare wall. 'One of you guys take the first turn,' I said. 'I'm fine here.'

25.

As it turned out, none of us actually slept, or not to begin with at least. Nobody spoke for a few moments, and the quiet of this new room asserted itself, made all the more obvious by the faint chatter filtering in from outside. As before, the hubbub sounded cheerful.

'What's the deal with these guys?' asked Xander. 'They're crooks, yet they step ashore in broad daylight to a hero's welcome. They parade us – stolen children – through the streets and nobody gives a damn.'

'It's not quite as simple as that,' said Mo.

'On one level – the most basic, obvious, incontrovertible one – it definitely is,' said Amelia.

'I'm with Amelia on this,' I said.

'I'm sure you are,' said Mo. 'And don't get me wrong, I don't want to defend them. But you have to understand them.'

'That's an easy way to overcomplicate things,' I muttered.

'Hear him out,' said Amelia.

'My country, Somalia, is a difficult place,' said Mo. 'For many years there was civil war here, and the fighting continues today. We have attacked ourselves from within, and this has meant we have been unable to defend ourselves properly from outsiders.'

'Whose problem is that?' I couldn't help saying.

'Right now, it's yours,' Mo said quietly, before continuing. 'But it is also a big problem for all of us, including our fishermen. Without a navy to protect our waters, outsiders took advantage. Big industrial fishing boats from other countries took our fish. This meant fewer fish for us. People on the coast grew poor and went hungry. Many pirates started out as fishermen. With nothing left to catch they put their knowledge of the ocean to other uses.

'First, they began hijacking foreign fishing vessels, as much to scare others away as to steal the boats and fish. Then they grew bolder and, with the help of ex-soldiers, they started targeting big international cargo ships. The companies who owned them paid ransom monies for the release of their cargo and to free their employees. For a time, the seas here were a virtual no-go area. Soon the international community fought back however, sending warships to patrol the seas. US and Chinese navy boats, fully armed, and willing to shoot and kill. Many pirates died.'

'My heart bleeds for them,' said Xander.

'But in the meantime, you see, the coastal communities had benefited. The pirates spent money ashore; markets thrived. It's the same the world over: wealth creates wealth, at least locally. Also, since the pirates had scared away the foreign fishing boats, the fish came back, and the seas grew plentiful again.'

I thought of Mum and her environmental crusade. Protecting coral reefs was top of her list, but she was also striving to ensure marine diversity and looking after fish stocks. To think that her efforts were in any way aligned with what the pirates were doing, however inadvertently, by defending their seas, made a sick sort of sense.

Mo went on: 'With the return of the fish, local fishermen made record catches. They earned money and others did too. People had enough to eat again.'

'It's like Robin bloody Hood,' I said.

'I do not know this . . .' said Mo.

A shot of something close to pleasure went through me: the boy hadn't heard of *everything* then.

'English folk hero,' said Amelia. 'Proto-Marxist. Robbed the rich, gave proceeds to the poor, against a backdrop of exploitative taxation.'

'That's one way of telling the story,' muttered Xander.

Mo ignored him and addressed Amelia. 'Yes, I remember now. The subject of many successful film interpretations. Errol Flynn, Kevin Costner, Russell Crowe, et cetera.'

The pleasure washing through me leaked away. I picked at a scab on my knee to divert myself.

'Also played by Sean Connery, and, most recently, Taron Egerton,' Amelia added.

'Yes, well, think of those films,' said Mo. 'The happiness of the poor people when Robin is among them. That's what it's like here. Our captors are seen as brave and helpful by the whole community.'

'Not least their mafia-style bosses,' said Amelia. 'Don't forget them.'

'I haven't,' said Mo. To me and Xander he explained, 'The men who risk everything to steal boats – small ones these days, since the big ships are so heavily defended – are not acting alone. They have backers. Rich men ashore who put up the money for their fuel and weapons. They expect and receive a big return on their investment. There is even an informal stock exchange selling shares in piracy operations! The pirates themselves only see a slice of the proceeds from their endeavours. Everyone knows this. They are not regarded as greedy thieves, more the defenders of our waters, men prepared to put their lives on the line to help rebuild this country.'

'By "endeavours" you mean stealing other people's property, kidnapping children to ransom, and killing innocent civilians,' I growled.

'Yes. As I say, it's complicated. Let me leave you with this. The Somali word for pirate is *burcad badeed*, which means ocean robber –'

'Sounds about right,' I interrupted.

'Yes, but the pirates themselves refer to what they do as *badaadinta badahor*, which translates as something like "saviour of the sea".'

I punctured the silence that followed this little lecture with a snort, but the awkward truth was that Mo's explanation did make sense of what I'd witnessed that afternoon. These guys had no reason to skulk about. At least not for the most part. Presumably there was *somebody* responsible for policing this bit of Somalia, but whoever it was obviously didn't trouble the pirates unduly. They had the support of the locals, that much was clear, and they were relying upon them to keep our location a secret for now.

It was an odd feeling, to think that a whole town was fine with our incarceration. Odd and unpleasant. If I could break us out of this room and run down the street shouting 'Help!' I'd likely be gathered up and handed straight back to Barrel-man again. Just as the pirates had used the Indian Ocean as the mother of all moats, they now had the land and everyone in it to contain us. Jumping overboard – for now at least – would be as pointless here as it had been at sea.

26.

They moved us inland the following day, but not before the stunt with the newspapers. I'd been wondering when it – or something like it – would come. Seemed they'd been waiting for a decent internet connection before making their ransom demand.

Mo, listening to the chat coming through the door, warned us what was coming. 'They're in no hurry,' he said. 'Right now, they allow your families to fear the worst. Then, when they make contact with proof-of-life, it's as if you've come back from the dead. This makes it more likely a big ransom is paid.'

I thought of the message I'd sent Mum and felt more determined than ever that these guys shouldn't earn a penny from our abduction. Did Xander and Amelia feel the same way though, still? I asked them again.

'Of course,' said Amelia straight away.

'Ideally,' added Xander.

Amelia immediately pointed out that he was leaving some

wriggle room with that word: 'There's nothing ideal about the situation.'

'I'm just not sure my parents will be content to sit back and wait for us to escape. Will yours?'

'My mum will do whatever Jack's mum advises,' she said matter-of-factly.

'The sooner we make a break for it, the sooner the problem will go away,' I said, as much to myself as anyone else.

Mo sucked air through his teeth when I said that. 'You must be careful with these men, on land as well as at sea,' he said. 'Be patient.'

'You would say that,' I couldn't help replying.

'We can't do much now anyway.' Xander, ever the diplomat, obviously wanted to head off any argument. He tapped at a breeze block. 'These are solid walls and that metal door must be an inch thick. We're not going to break out of here.'

'They won't be keeping us here for long,' said Mo, but immediately and annoyingly doused any spark of optimism by continuing with, 'However, where we're going next is just as secure in its own way.'

I pressed my shoulder blades into the solid brick wall, thinking again how beyond them, surrounding us, and making things worse, were a whole load of people apparently on the pirates' side.

'We're thinking about this the wrong way,' I said. 'Breaking out may not be an option, but persuading ourselves out could be.'

'Persuading?' said Amelia.

'Bargaining, negotiating, whatever.'

'You need something to bargain with for that to work.'

At this Amelia gave me one of her 'meaningful stares'. They're not very subtle. I had no idea what she meant by it, and was none the wiser when she gave an equally unsubtle micro-nod in Mo's direction before repeating the gesture.

What was she on about?

Unable to bear the fact that I hadn't cottoned on, she couldn't stop herself from spelling things out. 'Er, actually, I had one eye on the bargaining power trajectory from the beginning, as I'm sure you guessed.'

'Trajectory? Guessed?'

'With the anti-nausea tablets.'

'Come again?'

'When Xander was sick I dug out the motion sickness tablets I had in my bag. That didn't surprise you?'

I shrugged.

'Well, it should have, possibly because I've never suffered from motion sickness: not on the dive boat, not on any plane, and not during any of the million or so car rides we've shared since we were small.'

It was true. Neither of us ever gets car sick. We could both happily read a book in the back of Mum's Mercedes coupe while Mum, who drives pretty fast, raced along twisty country lanes.

'So, I assumed you'd see through that.'

'To what?' said Xander. 'I *was* actually sick. You gave me two pills. Not that they helped much.'

'Sure, but. You really don't get it, do you?' she said to me, exasperated.

I shrugged again.

'The pills were painkillers. Sorry, Xander, but they were. The point is: what else do you think might have been in that packet?'

'Beats me.'

At that she yanked off her trainer. The look on her face suggested any sane person would know the answer lay within it. In which case I'd have to plead insanity. I leaned forward, hands on my knees. Having given up hope on me she peeled off her trainer sock, turned it inside out, and shook four of the wedding rings we'd found on the seabed into her cupped palm.

I immediately glanced at Mo. He was wide-eyed in the gloom. Seeing that Amelia was reaching for her other trainer I quickly said, 'Don't bother, we get the picture.'

'Could have fooled me,' she replied, but with a smile.

I realised I was digging with my fingers at the softness running along the edge of my kneecaps, prying at them in my frustration. What was Amelia thinking, showing Mo the jewellery? How had I been so stupid as to let this happen? Already the boy's expression had changed, his quick surprise replaced with a more deadpan poker face. Valuable jewels, right there in the cell with us: how might he use that information?

'You don't seem particularly impressed,' Amelia said now.

Xander jumped in: 'Of course we are. With a bit of luck those will come in handy. But –' he couldn't keep a playful note out of his voice –'but why did you bring them to sea in the first place? Wouldn't they have been safer back in the hotel?'

'On the balance of probabilities, no,' said Amelia firmly. 'Valuables go missing from hotels the whole time. Those safes the hotel provides are unlockable with a master code. They have to be, otherwise daft tourists who forget their passcodes would forever be missing their flights home. It's hardly surprising stuff gets pinched from rooms every now and then: some of the poorest members of society, cleaning staff and so on, having their noses rubbed in the guests' excess day in, day out. They can't really be blamed for falling to such temptation. I mean, who wouldn't want to redress the balance?'

'Robin Hood again,' murmured Mo.

'And statistically speaking we were unlucky to be accosted by pirates,' Amelia went on blithely. 'That was unlucky –'

'Still is,' said Xander.

'Yes, but it doesn't alter the fact that my answer to your question is correct: probability-wise, the rings were safer with us than they would have been in the hotel. And my decision to bring them also turns out to have been expedient.' She glanced my way and, very annoyingly clocking that I didn't know what 'expedient' meant, went on: 'Useful in a practical sense, because they're more valuable to us as bargaining chips in this situation than they would have been in monetary terms ashore.'

As often happens with Amelia, everything she'd just

said was true, and yet it also missed the bleeding obvious. The rings were obviously valuable bargaining chips, if we played them carefully. But now Mo knew we had them, she'd effectively handed the advantage over to him. Because although he seemed trustworthy enough and was definitely putting on a good show of being on our side, he was – however reluctantly – one of the goddamn pirates!

27.

Shortly after Amelia undermined her very welcome revelation by spouting it in front of Mo, Flip-flops cracked the door to our cell and motioned for me to come out. Mo came too. I knew, because he had told us, that we were about to be photographed or filmed, and the three of us had agreed on the best way of turning that to our advantage.

The pirate-guard led me to a door at the rear of the house which gave out onto a dusty courtyard. Passing from the linoleum to dirt, the squelching sound of his flip-flops died. They flicked up little plumes of dust as he walked to the centre of the courtyard. Barrel-man handed up a newspaper, which Flip-flops passed to me.

Strangely enough the newspaper was in French, a copy of *Le Figaro*. I've admitted my French isn't good, but I nailed the days of the week at least, so I was able to translate the date on the front cover, which included the word *vendredi*.

While languages may not be my strong point, I'm good at keeping orientated in place and time. Today was Saturday, not Friday, so the newspaper was a day old. I didn't know whether to be impressed that the pirates had got hold of an international newspaper so soon after stepping ashore, or to pity them for not having found the most up-to-date copy. I don't suppose they thought a day mattered much in the scheme of things.

Aside from me, Mo and the two pirates, the courtyard was empty, of people that is. Two of the skinniest cats I've laid eyes on were stretched out on their sides in the shade of the eastern wall. They were both pretty much the same colour as the dirt they lay on, and they stayed so still throughout the process of me having my mug-shot taken – I couldn't even see them breathing – that I began to wonder whether they were dead.

There was no high-tech filming equipment, tripods or lights, and no fancy background of flags or banners or whatever, just Barrel-man with a mobile phone. He knew enough to move me to the other side of the courtyard, and therefore avoid capturing me as a silhouette, though.

The pirates wanted to send a message – pay up, or you won't see them again – to our parents with these snapshots and mini-films. Our task was to make the message mean something else. I was confident I could convey what I wanted to Mum. The first thing I did was grip both sides of the paper with tightly clenched fists. To Barrel-man, behind his smartphone, it probably looked like I was gripping the paper so tightly out of fear, but I reckoned Mum would pick up on the signal.

After my brother Mark died, whenever she's wanted to

reassure me without speaking out loud, she's squeezed her hands into two fists held just in front of her and added a quick smile-wink. I couldn't exactly time the wink, but narrowed one eye, and it was no problem to smile. I clenched that paper tight and gave the little lens on the back of the phone my cheesiest grin.

Barrel-man dropped the phone a few inches, looked over the top of it at me, and spat something at Mo.

'He's asking why you're smiling,' the boy said.

Without dropping my ridiculous grin, I told Mo to explain that ever since I was a small boy I'd smiled when nervous.

'He says don't be nervous or he'll give you something to be nervous about,' Mo reported after another exchange with the pirate.

I shook my head, as if trying to dislodge the smile, but made sure it was still in place when I looked back up. 'I can't help it,' I managed to say through the letterbox slit of my fixed grin.

Mo said something else to Barrel-man. I don't know what it was but it made the pirate's muscled shoulders shake with laughter. Out of the side of his mouth he spat a reply to Mo.

'He agrees: you look like you've wet your trousers,' Mo relayed.

Still smiling, I said, 'Whatever.' With the grin still in place, I hardened my one-eyed stare. Mum would get it.

Barrel-man, his thumb stabbing at the phone screen, had obviously switched to video mode now, since he gave Mo an order which the boy passed on as, 'He wants you to tell your parents we're treating you well but you're frightened of what we'll do if the money doesn't come through.'

I'd thought about this too. Still looking way more amused than afraid, I drawled, in the most sarcastic voice I could manage, 'Mum, these muppets are treating us *super*-nicely, but they're really, *really* frightening, obvs, and I'm *totally* scared of what will happen if you don't do *exactly* what they say, etc.'

When I use that tone of voice at home it drives Mum mad, but I knew it was my best means of reassuring her now: it's me at my most infuriatingly cocky, not remotely worried, never mind scared. I even risked a proper wink at the camera on the word 'etc.'

Barrel-man let that pass too. Perhaps he was focusing on the miniature version of me displayed on the phone screen rather than the real thing, and missed the wink; I don't know or care. As he lowered the phone I shot a sideways glance at Mo. He was staring at me with his mouth open a fraction.

'What?' I said.

Mo didn't say anything. I realised I was smiling with my eyes as well as my mouth now. He definitely got the sarcasm intended for Mum, but mercifully it seemed he wasn't about to point it out to Barrel-man. I softened towards him further. He seemed to be actually on our side for real. Why then wasn't he smiling back? How could he be so obviously in on the joke and apparently unable to see the funny side of it?

It dawned on me slowly. Barrel-man and his co-pirates might not pick up on what I'd done immediately, but if the video was out there then somebody else would spot it in the end.

And who would the pirates blame then? Me, sure, but also Mo for not pointing out what I'd done. He could pretend he hadn't cottoned on all he liked, but I knew they wouldn't believe him because over the past few days I'd seen the way they treated him. Like scum on the one hand, but scum they couldn't deny was useful: they knew he understood stuff they didn't. The way Barrel-man had walloped him in the boat said it all: we'll make use of your brain though we hate you for it. If they so much as suspected he'd let my sarcasm pass on purpose, they'd be harder on him than on me.

Mo was still staring at me, watching my expression change as I slowly realised what I'd done. It felt like the seconds after stubbing a toe, when I often want to kick whatever it was that I stubbed it on properly before the pain surges in. I wanted to apologise to Mo but instead I looked away from him.

28.

Mo was right in predicting the pirates would soon be moving us to a new location. Once Xander and Amelia had given their own little performances to Barrel-man – both of them reckoned they'd managed to pull off a bit of I'm-actually-OK insincerity – Flip-flops appeared in our little cell and said something to Mo which he translated as, 'Time for a meeting with the boss.'

To begin with I thought he meant the pirate captain. But he didn't. This boss character was nowhere nearby. To get to him we'd be making a journey by land. At least we'd have a chance to take a look at the scenery, I thought, but I was mistaken. Barrel-man appeared behind Flip-flops, a clutch of hessian bags in his sinewy hand. He tossed them down.

'You have to put these on, like this,' said Mo. He picked up a bag and, as if this sort of thing happened every day – who knows, perhaps it did? – he calmly pulled it down over his head.

Amelia, Xander and I looked at one another.

'Er, no thanks,' I said.

Barrel-man kicked the bags across the dusty floor at us.

'I'm not sure it's negotiable,' said Xander.

Mo, his voice small, said, 'Don't worry, it's not so bad.'

'It's all relative, I suppose,' said Amelia. She lifted a bag from the heap and, trying to put a brave face on things, gave me a weak smile before pulling the bag over her face. Xander followed suit.

They were right, of course. We didn't have a choice. Still, I was seething inside as I slotted my head into the last bag available. It was damp, scratchy, and it smelled of rotten fish. But sackcloth is porous, meaning we could breathe through these bags, despite the duct tape Barrel-man and Flip-flops used to secure them, noose-like, around our necks. Using the same tape, they also secured my hands behind my back again.

I'm not exactly claustrophobic, in that I can cope with being cooped up if necessary, but I don't like it. Plunged into the darkness of that sack, a fluttery feeling of panic rose up inside me. To head it off I closed my eyes, shutting myself inside my own head rather than staring into the blackness of the sack, and I forced myself to take long slow breaths.

Now that I couldn't see, my other senses pressed in. The horrible fish-stink of the bag blotted out everything else smell-wise. In fact, the smell was so strong it filled my mouth as well as my nose; I swear I could taste bad fish. The sackcloth was rough and damp against my cheeks, forehead and chin, and the noise of the room was muffled but still somehow louder than it had been: scuffling footsteps,

142

Barrel-man's jabbering, the deeper growl of Flip-flops talking to him.

Somebody took hold of my forearm. I pulled away at first, but the fingers tightened around my wrist again, pulling me forward. Blindfolded like that, we were taken outside one by one. Whoever was leading me was actually quite gentle. He had a palm in the small of my back and he steered me forward, making me feel less like I was about to nose-butt a wall. As I emerged into the compound, I heard a dog barking. It sounded close by. Outside, my guide led me twenty-two steps before turning me around to sit on the warm metal lip of a pickup's lowered tailgate. He leaned me backwards and swung my legs into the tray. Amelia was already in it; I rolled blindly onto her ankle.

'Ow!' she said.

'Sorry.'

'Oh, it's you.'

'Yeah. What about Xander?' I said.

'I'm coming, I think.' Xander's voice was off in the direction of the dog. But soon he was banging down into the corrugated metal beside me, and saying, 'That's kind of you, thank you very much,' with just enough sarcasm to make me smile under my hood. We jostled about until we were sitting in a line with our backs pressed to the same side of the pickup's hold. I was in the middle with Xander on my right and Amelia on my left.

Under my breath I said, 'We're together at least.'

Quietly, Mo chipped in: 'I'm here also.'

'Good,' I said, and I meant it. I was pleased to hear his voice.

The pickup's engine rattled to life and the tray shuddered beneath me. Doors banged shut. 'Brace yourselves,' I said, too late. We all lurched sideways into each other as the truck jumped forward. But we quickly righted ourselves. Until the pickup hit a pothole and swerved left, jumbling us all up again. The trouble was that, without being able to look at the scenery, let alone the road itself, I couldn't anticipate what was coming. None of us could. This was going to be an uncomfortable journey.

'How far is it?' I asked in the general direction of Mo.

'It depends.'

'If you've been there before, surely you must know,' I said.

Amelia snorted. 'Think about it,' she said. 'There could be traffic.'

'You reckon? It felt like we came ashore pretty much in the middle of nowhere. It's not like –'

Mo cut me off. 'Not traffic,' he said. 'But the roads. They are rough, damaged by the weather. Sometimes we have to go around.'

As if to underline Mo's point, at that moment the pickup lurched over what felt like a boulder-sized rut. I bounced clear off the tray and slammed back down into it with an audible – and painful – thump.

'What's the best-case scenario, journey-time-wise?' asked Xander, once we were rolling smoothly again. He didn't sound rattled, just interested, but he's always great at keeping calm.

'An hour and a half. Two, perhaps. If we're going where I think we are,' Mo replied.

'Where's that?'

Mo didn't reply at first. The pause became ominous. Eventually he said, 'Let's just wait and see, shall we.'

I have no idea how long the journey took. It was like the storm again: with my head in that bag my sense of time evaporated. The physical battering the road and truck delivered as we bounced and jerked and thumped over what seemed to be never-ending sharp-edged rocks was all-consuming. In reality the tyres were probably just clattering across dried-out ruts, but it felt worse. I know it's stupid, but I began to suspect that the driver was hitting obstacles deliberately.

To begin with, sitting separately, I felt like I might actually be thrown clear of the truck. Why not let that happen? Help it, even, by jumping to my feet and leaping out. I thought about telling the others to do that with me but really, it would have been stupid. We couldn't see where we were jumping and for all I knew one of the guards was probably in the back with us, keeping an eye.

By sitting close we wedged ourselves together to ward off the smaller bumps, but every now and then the pickup hit what felt like a log, throwing all four of us (Mo had joined our little human chain the other side of Amelia) up in the air at once and slamming us back down onto the ribbed metal tray with a steel-band crescendo *b-b-bang*.

Nobody complained.

In fact, when we spoke at all, we tried to make light of the hardship.

Xander's fake indifference rubbed off on the rest of us.

145

We said, 'Nice!' and 'Great!' and 'Bring it on!' instead of 'Ow!' and 'Damnit!' and 'I can't take much more!'

And it helped. When the pickup eventually jerked to a halt, I felt like I'd spent a day inside an industrial tumble drier, but I hadn't cracked. None of us had. Xander simply said, 'Well, that was fun,' and we waited beneath the beating sun, frightened, yes, but ready to face whatever would happen to us next.

29.

Somebody said something and Mo relayed it. 'Sit still, very still,' he said.

I waited, unable to decipher what was happening.

Xander said, 'Thanks so much. No, really.'

Then a hand gripped my shoulder and pulled me round. Fingers lifted the hem of the sack at the base of my throat. There was a ripping noise. Light broke in and a knife blade, carrying on past the duct tape and up into the hessian, passed a centimetre from my nose. Whoever it was yanked the sack – and a clump of my hair – clean off my head and tossed it aside. Blinking blindly, I followed Xander's example, murmuring, 'Too kind.'

Amelia went for a more direct approach. When she realised what was happening, she hissed, 'Be careful, will you, idiot!'

Happily, Barrel-man was wielding the knife and he didn't pick up on the insult. He cut Mo out of his hood last, then freed our hands and stood back from the truck while we got down and shook ourselves loose and adjusted to the brightness.

If I'd thought the little fishing port where we'd come ashore was the middle of nowhere, I was mistaken. Compared with this place, that was a metropolis. It had some proper buildings at least. We were in scabby bush here, with nothing nearby except a clutch of ragged-looking tents. The biggest one, nearest the truck, had no ridge pole. This gave it a deflated look.

A man emerged from between the tents. He was slight, about thirty years old, and he was wearing smart military fatigues. Despite the dusty surroundings his boots gleamed and his shirt was pressed. His scalp was also gleaming, oiled and as clean shaven as a conker. Tucked up under his left arm was a little black stick, a baton in fact, and he waved this in Barrel-man's direction as he approached.

Barrel-man took a deferential step backwards. The muscles in his neck were rigid. He said something quietly to the new guy, who ignored him in favour of looking us over.

'Good morning. Welcome,' he said. His mouth smiled but his eyes were unreadable. 'My name is General Sir.'

'General Sir what?' said Amelia.

'General Sir,' the man repeated, his cold smile still in place.

Amelia drew breath to say something else but I coughed and she got the message.

'Please,' said General Sir. 'You must be thirsty. Hungry. Come this way.'

Flanked by Barrel-man, the pickup driver and Flip-flops – the pirate captain appeared not to have made the journey with us – we four kids traipsed along in General Sir's wake, skirting the shabby tent towards a clearing among the thorny, head-high bushes that seemed to be a speciality of this dust-bowl place. As well as thorn bushes, there were flies. Lots of them. They buzzed around my head and tried to land on my face. I waved them away constantly. There were people scattered around this clearing too. Quite a few, in fact. General Sir led us briskly along. Distracted by the flies, it took me a moment to realise that the people were children.

'What is this place?' Amelia asked loudly.

Mo said, 'This is General Sir's camp.'

'Who's he when he's at home?' asked Xander.

Mo looked confused. 'At home he's the same as –'

'It's just an expression,' Amelia explained, swiping at a fly. 'It means who is he? These insects . . .' She whisked another away with her fingertips.

'You'll get used to them,' said Mo.

I doubted him, particularly as at precisely that moment a fly, its buzzing suddenly loud, landed just inside my ear. I shook my head hard to dislodge it and missed the first half of what Mo said next. It ended with, '. . . what he calls his covert operations.'

'What operations?' asked Amelia.

General Sir, having arrived at a blackened fire pit surrounded by scattered picnic furniture, spun on his heel. A few tendrils of smoke rose lazily behind him. He seemed to be waiting to hear Mo's response – how would the boy characterise what he, the General, was up to? – but Mo decided against giving an explanation for now. This seemed to please General Sir. He waggled the end of his baton at Mo and gave him a tiny nod of approval.

General Sir turned aside to Barrel-man and Flip-flops and had a quiet word with them. I watched closely and saw General Sir slip Barrel-man a thick brown envelope. Barrel-man didn't look inside it, just tapped the corner of the envelope against his forehead before shoving it unceremoniously into his back pocket. At which General Sir said something that had to do with Mo. I've no idea what it was, just that it made the pirates glance his way.

General Sir shook his head as he spoke; it sounded like he was explaining a sad fact. When he finished, he spread out his hands in a take-it-or-leave-it gesture, in response to which Barrel-man took a few quick steps our way and struck Mo hard across the face. The boy reeled, dropped to one knee, then slowly stood back up, keeping his head lowered.

General Sir spoke sharply to Barrel-man. It felt as if an argument would erupt between them. But then he softened and shrugged again, the beginnings of a smile playing on his lips. He burst out laughing. From the way the pirates joined in, it was clear they had to. Everyone laughs at the boss's jokes.

'Looks like I'm staying here with you,' Mo murmured. 'But why?'

'The videos. General Sir has seen them. He asked why you were not sincere. It was my fault, apparently.'

Mo rubbed the side of his head. Again, I felt bad about our stunt. Something didn't add up though. 'But why were they laughing?' I asked.

'Because General Sir is happy that the films, as proof-of-life, will work anyway. He is unconcerned and for that everyone is grateful.'

When Flip-flops, Barrel-man and General Sir had finished their conversation they all shook hands and the pirates set off back in the direction from which we'd come without giving Mo, or indeed any of us, a second look.

I know it's ridiculous but I was almost sorry to see them go.

Who the hell was this guy, and why were they leaving us with him?

Mo knew, I supposed.

General Sir now waved in the direction of the flung furniture – plastic chairs, mostly, on their sides or backs in their dirt. 'Please, sit down,' he said.

This was more of an order than an invitation. We did as we were told. There was a dog asleep on its side in the middle of the furniture, a big ragged-looking hound of some sort. It opened one eye as I picked up a chair, saw General Sir beside me, and levered itself up warily. Flies rose from its dusty fur. General Sir helped it on its way with a kick. The dog's tail curled up under its belly as it quickened away.

I set the chair straight and realised it was almost identical to the one I have at my desk in my bedroom back in England. This one was dustier, and a whole lot further from whichever Ikea it had started out in. Something about the familiarity of that chair made me realise how far from home I was, and I thought of Mum. A terrible lurching sensation swept through me as I sat down.

General Sir tucked his little baton back up under his armpit, sheathing it there for now. He looked us over blankly. What did he want with us, and why was he somehow more menacing than the pirates he had taken us from?

30.

'Now that you are our guests, we must offer you something to eat,' General Sir said. 'It's the first rule of hospitality here.' He turned and spoke to the group of kids by the fire pit and one of the boys, aged around eleven, jumped instantly to his feet and ran off in a hurry.

General Sir watched him go, then looked back at us with the same fixed smile. 'Jamal won't be a minute,' he said.

In fact, the boy was gone for what felt like an age, possibly because General Sir just stared at us without saying anything else until he returned. Eventually Jamal came back accompanied by another, even smaller boy, who couldn't have been more than nine. They had a bowl in each hand. Without meeting our eyes, these two boys approached the four of us and offered us each a helping of the food they'd fetched from wherever.

Xander said, 'Thank you,' taking his.

Amelia and I followed suit.

Mo said nothing.

The boys backed away.

I looked down at my bowl. It contained grey gloop, the consistency of mashed potato crossed with porridge. Amelia, frowning, said – quite loudly – 'Do you think they'll bring us some spoons?'

'I somehow doubt it,' said Xander, nodding at Mo, who had already pinched a blob of whatever it was between fingers and thumb and begun to knead it into a ball of sorts. Once satisfied the stuff would hold together, he popped the ball into his mouth. Evidently, he'd eaten this dish before, but whether or not he liked it I couldn't say: his face gave nothing away.

The gloop was stickier than it looked, a viscous paste. It clung to my fingertips. I was nowhere near as adept as Mo at making a bite-sized lump, and I can't say I was expecting much when I eventually tasted it. In that I wasn't disappointed. I thought: wet cardboard, with added grit. Perhaps that's actually what it was?

I glanced at Xander. He was chewing mechanically. When he caught my eye he pulled a micro-gag expression, puffing out his cheeks for a nanosecond. Unfortunately – but true to form – Amelia spelled out what we were all thinking.

'This is revolting,' she muttered, and went on more loudly: 'I'm afraid I can't eat it. I'm not hungry enough.'

General Sir said, 'You will be, you will be.' There was no anger in his voice. He waved Jamal forward. The boy was wearing tatty jeans cut off at the knee and the natural dark brown of his lower legs, like his bare feet, was tinted red with dust. It was only as he retreated with Amelia's more-or-less untouched bowl that I noticed he had a handgun sticking out of his waistband in the small of his back. I flinched. Jamal definitely wasn't more than eleven or twelve years old. The shock of seeing his gun made me spoon up the gunk in my bowl with my fingers more rapidly. I ate without tasting, or indeed chewing much; I just thumbed the paste into my mouth and swallowed it down.

Seeing that Mo and I had finished, Jamal's little helper approached us again carrying a metal bucket half filled with water. Sunk within it was a pink plastic beaker. He scooped the beaker full and handed it to Mo, who drank. I did the same, not allowing myself to question where the water had come from or how clean it might be. I was thirsty. We all were: everyone took their fill from that same cup.

Satisfied that he'd fulfilled the first rule of hospitality, as he put it, General Sir dismissed Jamal and his friend with a flick of his thin wrist. They didn't go far, just retreated beyond the fire pit to join a group of kids who had gathered, apparently, to marvel at us.

'I expect you're tired after the journey here,' General Sir said, looking over the tops of our heads. 'So, make yourselves comfortable and I'll be back later, once you've rested. We'll make a start then. OK?'

I waited until General Sir had retreated among the bushes before asking Mo, 'What did he mean by that? Why are we here? And what is this place anyway?'

'It's a training camp,' Mo said. 'For child soldiers. But I can't believe he'd want *you* for *that*.'

31.

'Child soldiers?' said Xander. 'You're not serious?'

'Why wouldn't he be?' Amelia asked.

I had my eyes fixed on the group of kids watching us. Jamal was among them, and I noticed that he wasn't the only boy with a gun. Two of the others had weapons of one sort or another that I could see. The biggest kid squatting in the middle of the group was holding what looked like a semi-automatic rifle across his knees, and that scrawny boy wearing a military beret and sitting off on his own was actually cradling a musket.

'What are they staring at?' asked Amelia.

'Us,' said Xander.

'Come,' said Mo, and drew us into the shade of a big thorn bush. We plonked ourselves close to him, and not just because the patch of shade was small. We needed answers, and Mo had them. Xander was twisting at his own fingers and Amelia was doing the fast-blinking thing she does when anxious. Nobody likes not knowing what's going on but she really can't bear it; I wasn't surprised when she blurted out, 'Who do these kids fight for? And where do they come from?'

'All over,' said Mo. 'Places like my village, or the thousands of other villages like it. Anywhere people are poor. General Sir picks kids from the streets, the fields, even takes them from school.'

'From schools?' said Xander. 'You're kidding?'

'No. If supply is low from the streets, kids already abandoned, he sends out a raiding party to take some who have a home. They go into schools and steal children from the yard or classroom. If the teachers object . . . well, they risk their lives if they do that. And they know it, so they don't, mostly.'

I let this sink in, imagined myself in a lesson at school, chemistry, say, doing a stupid drawing of a Bunsen burner, trying to concentrate, knowing that at any moment a group of armed kids led by a man in uniform might barge in and tell the teacher the class was over, they were taking us off to war. Perhaps they'd be waving guns around, or even firing them in the air, to spell things out. I'm no fan of chemistry but even so.

'And who do they fight for?' Xander repeated.

'Ah, that's the thing with General Sir,' said Mo. 'His soldiers fight for anyone who wants them. This is his business, you see. He steals children for others to use. While they're here he gives them a little training with guns and explosives so they're more valuable, and then he sells them on to the militia, or the army, whoever will pay.'

'Which militia? Which army?' asked Xander.

Amelia couldn't help herself. 'Al-Shabaab, I'm guessing. That's the biggest militia group. Mainly they're in the south.'

'You mean roughly here,' I chipped in.

'Correct,' said Amelia.

Mo went on, 'But there are also other militia who don't much like the idea of sharia law, which Al-Shabaab wants to impose. And then you have the Kenyan army to the south, policing the disputed buffer zone between Kenya and Somalia. Plus of course the main force opposing them and Al-Shabaab, the Somali National Army. As the name suggests, that's the country's official army.'

'But surely the government's army doesn't recruit children?' asked Amelia.

Mo shrugged and said, 'It's not official but it happens. They pretend that the children don't actually fight, just cook and clean and help out, but that's not true. Both sides, and everyone in between, employ child soldiers. It's nothing new around here.'

I looked away from Mo. From this vantage point I made out a building a little way off in the scrub, down an incline to the north. It was a shack made out of scrap wood and cinder blocks. General Sir had gone off in that direction. I wanted to get my bearings in this new place as quickly as possible. Why? So that I could start plotting our escape, obviously.

The group of kids who'd been watching us by the fire pit had drifted along behind us. The big one, with the semi-automatic rifle, was closest. When I returned his stare, he held my gaze. Most people don't do that: nine times out of ten, if you look straight back at somebody who's watching you, they immediately look away. It unnerved me, the way he just stared back. Was he unhinged?

To be stuck a million miles from God-knew-where at the mercy of mental kids with guns made me gulp so hard my throat hurt. But I wasn't about to show my fear by blinking first. I stared back at that mean-looking boy soldier until he was finally distracted by one of the littler kids asking him a question.

There was something odd about this smaller boy's musket. The barrel was chipped, flaky with old paint. The gun was made out of wood, I saw; it was a fake. I nearly laughed when I realised that, but instead checked the big kid's gun, and when I confirmed that it was very real indeed the laughter dried up in my chest.

I'd lost track of time during our blindfolded journey but now noticed that I was squinting at the kids' guns. Dusk was falling. The nearer the equator you are, the faster that happens. The sun dropped out of the sky very quickly, showboating a blood-red sunset that seemed more or less to be over before it had begun.

Mo told us more about General Sir's operation as the sky darkened. Mo himself had been captured during a raid on his village by one of General Sir's patrols, four years ago. Because of Mo's cleverness (he didn't put it that way, of course, he called it 'usefulness' instead) he'd been spared the fate of most of the children who passed through the General's camp, so far at least. They were destined to fight at the front for the army or militia. But Mo's 'extra skills with languages et cetera' made General Sir loan him out to the pirates instead. Their exploits were a strand of the General's 'wider operation'. By this Mo meant that General Sir invested – both money and manpower – in the pirates' raids and took a chunk of the spoils. That's what we were, I realised: a share of the treasure. Mo called helping the pirates 'the easy option' and he wasn't joking.

'Do the other kids resent you for it?' Amelia asked.

'Why would they?' said Xander.

Mo shrugged. 'They know I'm expendable too. The thing with the blindfolds, for example. I have to wear one entering and leaving just like you. General Sir doesn't want any of the kids who pass through this camp to be able to find a way back to it, for obvious reasons.'

'Not obvious to me,' said Amelia.

'Child soldiers become dangerous men,' said Mo with a shrug. 'And they have reason to want revenge.'

Mo's face was silver. It was lit, I realised, by a sky bright with stars. I looked up at them for a moment and realised, gratefully, that the flies had gone.

When I looked back down General Sir was somehow right next to us, flanked by a couple of kids. I started. I hadn't heard him approach at all. But if he'd been listening to what Mo had told us he didn't let on. He simply said, 'You must be very tired after your journey. These may be helpful for your night's rest,' and motioned for the two boys to put down the basket they were carrying.

It contained blankets. He passed these around himself. The way he did it seemed courteous, attentive, *kind* even. I heard myself thanking him as if he'd done us a real favour. 'You're very welcome. Sleep well,' he replied, before retreating.

Though it could only have been about seven in the evening, General Sir was right. I was exhausted. This was hardly surprising given the ordeal of the day.

'Where do we sleep then?' I asked Mo. The thin blanket in my hands had a greasy feel to it. I waited for him to make a move, but he didn't. He wrapped his own blanket around his shoulders, rolled onto his side, and stretched out in the dirt instead.

'You're not serious,' said Xander. 'Isn't there room in one of the tents?'

'You can look,' said Mo. 'But they're generally full. Besides,' he said, nodding in Amelia's direction.

'Besides what?' said Amelia.

He didn't reply, but I understood what he left unsaid. I'd not seen another girl here. The group watching us were all boys. Amelia is more than capable of standing up for herself – among boys or girls – but still. I think she'd also worked out what Mo meant because she said, 'It's a good clear night, anyway,' in a very quiet voice and set about making herself comfortable with her blanket.

We lay in a line beneath the stars. Amelia was shivering beside me, and not because she was cold. I wanted to tell her that everything would be OK, but I knew I wouldn't be able to keep the fear out of my voice if I spoke, and that would only have made matters worse. I put a hand on Amelia's shoulder instead, squeezed it once, and lay there wondering how I'd ever plot us a way out of this horrendous mess.

32.

I slept without dreaming and woke up not knowing where I was. For a second I could have been at home under my duvet. It was a blissful thought. Immediately, however, reality came crashing in. Unlike the freshly laundered smell and feel of my duvet, the blanket currently pulled up under my nose was thin and greasy and smelled of old socks. Also, my bed is soft but the ground beneath me was hard as pavement. And whereas the only things staring at me when I wake up at home are the pictures on my bedroom walls (the closest one is of a tiger swimming across a lake: I've had it since I was small), now I was being stared at by eyes I did not recognise.

I jerked upright. 'What the hell are you looking at?' I said.

The eyes belonged to a boy of about ten. His head bobbed back on his shoulders but he didn't move away. Neither did the boy behind him or the one to his side. There were more! How long had they been sitting there watching us sleep?

Amelia was stretching and Xander had pushed himself up on one elbow, but Mo was the first of the others to sit up and take in what was going on. He muttered something to the boys. His tone was kinder than mine and I immediately felt embarrassed at having barked at them. They slunk off.

Breakfast was the exact same meal as the day before, brought to us by another two boys, who came from the direction of General Sir's shack. Amelia refused to eat it again. I wanted to encourage her to try but understood her well enough to know that it would just backfire.

As the rest of us finished eating, General Sir appeared. The dog I'd disturbed the previous day was with him, together with another, more wolf-like hound. He had the big, menacing-looking kid who'd stared me down the day before with him as well. Mo later told me his name was Kayd. The boy and the dogs looked dusty and flyblown; by contrast General Sir looked immaculate again, his uniform pressed, his head newly shaven and oiled, and as usual he had his little baton under his arm. I wanted to rip it from him and snap it in two, but something about the man – the fact he could ship us off to war, probably – made it very difficult to be anything other than polite to him.

I returned his greeting with a 'good morning' of my own. Apart from his baton it seemed that General Sir's policy was to carry nothing at all. Instead he had his minions lug stuff around in his wake. Kayd had an armful of spades and picks. At General Sir's instruction he dropped these heavily in front of us and stepped away, a glint in his eye.

'As Mo knows, I encourage new recruits to make a start with some light work. Today I thought you might like to help clear the new field.'

Never mind the 'encourage' and 'thought you might like' stuff, there was nothing negotiable about the General's offer. Without making comment Mo picked up the nearest shovel.

It was strange, but the whole thing reminded me of the way kids – myself included – behave when they first start at school: they follow the lead of whoever looks like they know the ropes. Mo had been here before. It seemed best to copy him. As I did so it occurred to me that General Sir keeping Mo with us would be a good tactic to make us behave.

We walked through the scrub for about forty minutes. Already the heat of the day was building. The dust we kicked up smelled like something baked. The scrubland was low-lying and flat at first, but in time it dipped away and bigger bushes sprang up. We were headed towards a meagre stream. Before we got there, we came upon an open stretch in which a number of boys – and, I noticed with relief, for Amelia's sake – a few girls were already at work.

We'd made this trip following General Sir. He didn't walk so much as glide ahead with his stupid baton tucked under his arm, and none of us had spoken to him. Once we'd stopped at the head of the field, however, Amelia stuck her hands on her hips and said, 'What on earth is the point of making us dig this field?'

General Sir spun around, flashing his mirthless smile. 'Once it is cleared, we can use it to plant crops.'

'Of course,' said Amelia. 'But why *us*? No offence, but aren't we worth more to you than that?'

I winced. Amelia was trying to sound sure of herself but the fear in her voice came through all the same. General Sir's smile remained in place. 'Work is good for everyone. You included!' he said. He looked around and pointed his baton-tip at an area that had yet to be cleared. 'Mo will explain what to do, but essentially I would like you to work here. Understood?'

He didn't wait for a reply, just ground another dimple in the dirt with his heel and marched off, not in the direction we'd come from, which was from the north, but south-east. We watched him disappear, the dogs trailing behind him. Off he went, gliding with a purpose, like a parking warden doing his rounds.

'He wants us to dig about in the dirt?' said Xander, incredulous.

'Yes,' said Mo. 'He tries out everyone the same way. If they make good workers they progress.'

'To what?' I asked.

'Soldiering,' said Mo matter-of-factly. 'It's a test.'

'A test I don't want to pass,' said Xander.

More quietly, Amelia added, 'Me neither.'

Mo had taken up one of the tools. It was a sort of pick with a wide blade. He tested the weight of it and said, 'Nobody does, but even so . . .' He held the tool out to Xander.

Xander said, 'I don't want a goddamn axe!'

'It's actually a mattock,' said Amelia.

For some reason the fact that she couldn't help herself correcting him, even here, now, made me laugh, and that broke the tension. Xander smiled with me.

Mo said, 'It is unwise to upset General Sir. If he tells us to clear this area we should do as he says, trust me.' His eyes were wide, pleading.

I picked up a shovel and said, 'Well, we don't want to disappoint him, do we.'

Following my lead, Xander took the mattock from Mo. He got the picture.

'What happens when General Sir is upset?' Amelia asked.

Mo had picked up the remaining two tools, a spade and a sort of crowbar. He held them up for Amelia to choose between. 'It's just wise to do as he asks,' he said, 'or . . .'

'Or what?'

Mo sighed. 'Or else.'

So, we cleared the field. Or some of it, at least. I have to admit the lion's share of what we achieved was due to Mo. He seemed not to notice the heat, which built through the morning despite the cloud cover. We were lucky it was an overcast day. The full glare of the sun would have been unbearable.

Xander was wearing a shirt over his T-shirt. He took it off and we ripped it up into sections we could dunk in the dirty little stream, then tied them around our heads. The wet strips cooled us down a little and had the added benefit of keeping off the flies, which were back with a vengeance. I tied mine with a tail I could flick to disturb them. Still, every minute or so I had to stop what I was doing to wave the ever-present fly-cloud away.

Mostly we were uprooting small bushes. This involved digging round the base of each plant and then yanking it free. Since the earth was hard we had to break it up with the crowbar first. Then we gouged and stabbed at the clutching roots with the mattock, pickaxe and spade. Once they were properly exposed the crowbar was good for levering the roots up and snapping them clear. And after we'd ripped the bush out and lugged it away, we broke up the remaining soil, cleared it of as many weeds and stones as possible, and levelled it off.

I hadn't been working more than an hour before the first blister rose across my palm. Changing tools with Xander stopped it from getting immediately worse, but before long the mattock was rubbing at the base of my thumb, and when I swapped, the crowbar made it worse.

By lunchtime, when General Sir reappeared, dogs in tow again, my hands were a mess, I was filthy, everything else ached, the flies were maddening, and I was boiling up inside and out. I know Amelia and Xander were in a similar state.

None of us had admitted it out loud though. That was the deal: we were stronger together if none of us cracked. But I'd spotted Amelia wincing as she worked and Xander's grunts of effort now had a pained edge to them. Only Mo appeared genuinely unconcerned.

Between us we'd cleared a patch of earth roughly half the size of a tennis court. General Sir took it in with a glance. I was annoyed to find that I genuinely cared whether we'd met his expectations, and not just because I feared what Mo's 'or else' might entail. Somehow the man's approval mattered to me.

'Good work,' he said, and the sense of relief I felt disgusted me. 'But hard, yes. You look tired. Come!'

And with that he led us back to the camp. This time he

took us straight to his shack, however. I heard engine noise as we approached but there was no vehicle in sight. It took me a moment to realise the sound was coming from a generator. That's what was powering the little fridge in the corner of the single room into which General Sir had ushered us.

The room was as neat as its occupant. No flea-ridden dogs were allowed in here. There was a cot bed with a blanket, the corners of which were tucked in, next to a little table and a single wooden chair. On the table stood a laptop computer, plugged into an extension cord and connected to a mobile phone. The laptop's screen was up.

With the air of a host at Christmas, General Sir took four cans of what turned out to be orangeade from his fridge and handed them round. In my entire life I have never appreciated a cold drink more, and the gratitude I felt towards the General sickened me further.

I edged closer to the little table as I drank, just a step, but enough to glance at what was on the laptop screen. What I glimpsed made no sense at all. Had the orangeade gone to my head?

Half a step closer I dared to take a longer look. I knew that face because I'd seen it on a screen before. Then, it had been on Mum's laptop, in the swanky resort, a world away from here. But this was the same photograph, I was sure, of a man with a fighter's square chin and wide-spaced, watchful eyes set beneath a determined brow.

The face was as familiar to me as it was foreign. I had no idea who he was, but he was the same guy Mum had been in touch with, definitely. It was *him*.

33.

General Sir gave us the rest of the day off. He acted as if he was being kind to us because we were 'new', but immediately undercut that by saying, 'You'll soon get used to things,' making it clear he intended to put us to work again before long. As soon as we were alone again outside, I brought up the photograph with Amelia and Xander.

'Whose face was it?' Amelia asked.

'That's the thing. I don't know.'

'Well, if it was on General Sir's screen as well as your mum's, whoever it is must be famous,' said Xander. 'They were probably on news sites. Whoever it is must be an actor or a politician.'

'Or a sportsman,' added Amelia helpfully. 'Was he swinging a golf club or anything?'

'No!' I said. 'And it wasn't a newspaper site. The guy is in Mum's contacts. She was messaging him.'

'Yeah, but your mum knows some pretty influential people,' reasoned Xander.

'So does General Sir,' added Mo quietly.

'Really,' I snapped. 'Mum and General Sir. A humanitarian from Surrey and a child-slave-trafficking warlord from Southern Somalia. I bet they have loads of friends in common.'

'Either way the coincidence isn't Mo's fault,' said Amelia. 'And unless you have a better hypothesis it seems the most likely solution to the mystery.'

Xander could see I was rattled by this suggestion. 'Yeah, but perhaps the most likely explanation,' he suggested, 'is that you've made a mistake. You could have seen two similar faces and jumped to the wrong conclusion. My head's definitely been fried today by the heat and the flies and the back-breaking –'

'No!' I cut him off more loudly than I'd intended. Lowering my voice, I went on. 'It's the same guy, I'm sure of it.'

'If you say so,' said Amelia, making no attempt to sound convinced.

Whatever the truth, I could do little about it for now. If – no, *when* – I made it back to Mum, well, I could ask her then. I was mulling over this unsatisfactory conclusion when General Sir reappeared from the shack. 'Another treat for you all!' he said, and slung a tattered kit bag into the centre of our dusty circle.

'What's in it?' Amelia asked.

'Home!' he said, and waved at the bag with his baton, as if about to do a magic trick.

By 'home' he meant a moth-eaten tent. I could have punched him for the insult in this, but again the meagre good news that we wouldn't have to spend another night out in the open did in fact come as a relief. Having revealed his generous gift General Sir sauntered off, leaving us to erect it.

This was easier said than done, mostly because the tent was incomplete. Specifically, part of one of the A-frame legs was missing, though it took me a while to work that out. I figured it out eventually, just as Mo, who'd wandered off when we unpacked the tent, came back. He was carrying a stick. I knew instantly why: he'd taken one look at the contents of the kit bag, identified the problem, and set off to solve it.

As we watched, he ripped strips from the end of that stick with his teeth until it was thin enough to ram into the open end of the A-frame joint. He'd even estimated the correct length of the missing pole. I stood back, noticing that he let Amelia and Xander do the easy bit: pull the canvas into place, peg it down over the groundsheet, hammer in the pegs with a rock, and tighten up the guy ropes.

When up, the tent was only slightly bent. Mo had repaired it with a stick. Yet he made nothing of it, just went off to gather up the blankets, trudged back with them, and dropped them onto the groundsheet. We stood quietly for a moment.

Then a bird sheared down. We all ducked. Eagle, kite, hawk: whatever kind of bird it was, it scythed through the air like an axe-head, only veering away at the last moment.

'Why did it do that?' asked Amelia.

'Probably checking out the new real estate,' said Xander.

'Yeah, good job mending it,' I said to Mo eventually.

'No problem.'

'Does General Sir always give out incomplete shelters?' asked Amelia.

'Often, yes. It's another of his stupid tests.'

I couldn't help admiring Mo in that moment, yet something about his easy mastery of just about everything sent a chill through me even as I tapped his closed fist with my own.

34.

We spent the next few days locked in an awful cycle: gut-busting work punctuated by bowlfuls of that terrible sludgy food – there was nothing else, so even Amelia soon caved in and ate it – and nights of poor sleep. We were filthy and exhausted and everything ached. General Sir gave us some woven mats, but they were wafer thin and spread on packed dirt so they offered no comfort. By about day six I felt like a zombie. I was so weak and tired that I could barely think straight.

'It's deliberate,' I said to Xander as we trudged back from the field after another gruelling spell of stump-hacking.

He waved at the ever-present cloud of flies and said, 'What is?'

'This routine. It's designed to wear us down.'

'Break us, more like,' said Amelia.

'You're right, Jack,' Mo explained. 'It's what he does with all new recruits – makes everyone so tired they become, what's the word . . .'

'Compliant?' Amelia suggested.

'Unable to think for themselves, more likely to give in and do what they're told.'

'That's what it means, more or less,' Amelia agreed.

'Compliant then. And less likely to run away,' said Mo.

'I'd have trouble running a bath,' said Xander. 'I'm not sure I've got the strength to turn on the taps.'

'It's the food's fault,' said Mo. 'There isn't much goodness in it.'

This made sense. The best that could be said for the sludge was that it filled a hole, but it didn't exactly fill me with energy. With all the physical work, I'd lost weight. We all had. The dents above Amelia's collarbones had deepened and Xander was definitely thinner in the face. General Sir was literally working us to the bone. I'd thought it best to take stock of our situation before mounting an escape, but maybe I'd made a mistake.

'If we don't make a run for it soon, we'll be too weak to try,' I said in the dark of the tent that night.

'I wouldn't risk it,' Mo replied.

'Why not?'

'You wouldn't be the first to attempt to get away. I've seen what happens when people try.'

'What?' Amelia asked, genuine fear in her voice.

'General Sir makes an example,' said Mo. 'Anyway, if you wait it out, sooner or later he'll get his ransom, and then he'll free you himself. He's making your parents sweat with this waiting, driving up his price. But he'll want the money eventually. Just do as he says and be patient.'

'That's probably good advice,' said Xander.

Deep down, I knew he was right. But still: I'd told Mum not to pay the ransom for a reason. I'd got myself into this mess. It was up to me to get myself out of it. I couldn't just sit there waiting for help.

'We should try at night,' I said, as much to myself as the others. 'Turn in as usual, then sneak off in the dark. Head south. We may not know exactly where we are but the Kenyan border can't be that far away.'

Mo gave a little snort. 'If it was that easy,' he said.

'We won't know unless we try,' I said. 'If we can get far enough away before anyone notices, they'll not be able to track us down.'

'I wouldn't bet on it. You've noticed the dogs in camp?'

'Yes. They seem harmless enough.'

'They're tracking dogs. They like nothing more than to chase a scent.'

Amelia piped up then with, 'Ah, the tent.'

'What about it?' said Xander.

'It smells of us.'

The penny dropped. Far from doing us a favour, by giving us a tent and blankets General Sir had impregnated them with our scent.

'That's right,' said Mo. 'We may not be caged here but the dogs are a sort of fence. You could have a whole day's head start and it would make no difference. They'd still catch up.'

'There's a chance we could make it,' I muttered. 'And anyway, think about it, what's the worst that could happen? You said it yourself, we're valuable to him. If he hunts us

175

down with the dogs, he'll hardly let them rip us apart. He'll just haul us back here to work and wait again.'

'You, maybe,' said Mo quietly. 'It's a chance you could take. But not me. Nobody is about to pay a ransom for me.'

Xander tried to reassure him otherwise, saying, 'You're valuable in a different way,' but it didn't stop me regretting what I'd said. What a selfish idiot. We lay there in silence for a bit. I was wishing I'd said nothing at all about trying to escape. I should have waited until I had a proper plan. Talking about something you want before you've got a sensible way of achieving it only makes whatever it is less likely to happen, in my experience.

'When you say he makes an example of people, what do you mean?' Amelia asked, her voice small.

Mo didn't answer her directly. Instead he said, 'I'm tired. We should try to get some sleep.'

35.

The following afternoon, walking back from the stump-field, we came upon a bunch of new recruits doing a form of military training. It seemed mostly to involve poking wooden guns into sandbags, crawling around in the dirt on all fours, and running on the spot holding something heavy: a lump of wood, an old tyre, a breeze block.

There was a bored air to all of these activities. The teenager supervising looked half asleep and none of the other kids were putting in much effort.

But further on from this weary circus we passed another little gathering learning how to use real guns. A boy about my age was showing a semi-automatic rifle – Mo said later that it was an AK-47, one of the few working guns General Sir kept under lock and key – to three boys who looked about ten.

I slowed my pace to watch. The older kid was acting very cool, the big man at ease with a deadly weapon. He took the magazine off the gun, jabbed his finger into the hole, waggled it about, then flipped the cartridge over and slotted it back into place. With no warning at all he lifted the gun to his hip and pulled the trigger, firing it at nothing in particular.

I had an immediate flashback and saw chips of fibreglass ripping from Pete's beautiful boat. The harsh metallic sound of the gun, and the casualness of the kid unleashing it, took me straight back to Flip-flops and Barrel-man.

We were in the middle of nowhere here but bullets fly miles. The four or five this boy had shot off could have ended up anywhere. As I watched, he removed the magazine again and held it and the gun up for the ten-year-olds to inspect. For some reason all of the boys burst out laughing. Swap the AK-47 out of the picture and they could have been showing each other a stupid meme on a phone.

The big kid with the gun now handed both bits over to one of the ten-year-olds. Still in the grip of the joke, the little boy nevertheless managed to refit the magazine. It didn't matter that he was laughing; the gun gave him a sort of swagger. He was a skinny kid, couldn't have weighed more than forty kilos, and he was already wobbling about with the giggles, so when he copied his instructor and nonchalantly fired the semi-automatic from the hip the force of the recoil spun him backwards. He had no weight behind the gun and was completely off balance. Its muzzle swung our way.

Instinctively I ducked, yanking Amelia down with me. Both Mo and Xander dropped to the ground as well. It was a good job, because the little idiot still had his finger on the trigger and, whether he meant to or not, he pulled it again. With the rifle pointed at us! I swear the shot was louder with the gun aimed our way. A flash of orange flame burst from the barrel.

Mercifully, this second shot only knocked one person over: the kid who fired it. The recoil made him sit down on his bum in the dirt. He threw the assault rifle aside as if it was a live thing he couldn't trust. But he was still laughing. They all were. They thought it was hilarious. Even when Mo shouted at them, they kept at it with the giggles. Only as we stood up and dusted ourselves off did the little twit who'd nearly killed us glance down the track towards camp and abruptly shut up. Panic flared in his eyes.

General Sir was striding towards us. He'd clearly seen what had happened, and he looked furious. He said nothing until he was standing right over the boys. All four of them shrank before him. With one hand he grabbed the kid who'd nearly shot us, and he took hold of the teenage instructor with the other.

He had them by the hair. The teenager was nearly as big as General Sir, but neither he nor the little one resisted as the General banged their heads together, hard enough for the thwack to be audible.

It was almost funny: less than a minute beforehand they'd been tough guys with a gun, and now they looked like little kids in trouble. Both of them kept their eyes down for the short walk back to camp. We followed. The General led them purposefully. Clearly the punishment wasn't over.

'What's going to happen to them?' I asked.

'The pits, probably,' said Mo.

'What's that?'

'Come and see for yourselves.'

As the General peeled off behind his own quarters Mo led us along with him. General Sir took the two boys further into the bush. Quite a way, in fact. When he finally stopped, Mo raised a hand and we all stopped too.

General Sir had his baton out again. He pointed it at the teenage instructor and then at the ground. From where we were, it wasn't clear what he was jabbing at down there. But the boy knew what to do. He bent over and levered up a metal door set flush with the ground. Then he climbed into the hole beneath it and let the door clang shut.

The General knelt to work a long bolt into place across the top of the door, with a metal-on-metal shriek.

'What's down there?' asked Amelia, as the General made the smaller boy climb into his own hole in the ground.

'Nothing. That's the point.'

'Nothing?'

'They're just empty cages buried in the ground. Smallish cages. I think they were meant for animals. You can't stand up in them, or lie straight. You just have to sit there on your own until General Sir lets you out. It's dark in the pits and they get hot. He had them dug all the way out here so that anybody yelling doesn't disturb him back in camp.'

The little kid had shot at us accidentally and hurt nobody. To be buried in an underground cage for doing something stupid hardly seemed fair, particularly when the guy doing the burying was responsible for giving the boy in question an assault rifle in the first place.

'How long does he put people in there for?' asked Amelia. She gets claustrophobia. A punishment like that would be bad for anyone, but from the look on her face it was obviously her idea of hell.

'It depends on what you've done,' Mo replied. 'A day or two, normally.'

Xander shuddered. 'Is it his way of making an example of people who, say, get caught running away?' he asked.

'Yeah,' said Mo, looking at me. 'One of them.'

36.

Later that afternoon there was a commotion in camp. Two white Land Rovers rolled up in a dust cloud and crunched to a stop next to General Sir's shack. He materialised at once to greet whoever had come to pay us a visit, and in response to his barked order a group of kids immediately assembled beyond the vehicles. When I say assembled, I mean it; the boys, twelve of them in total, stood four abreast in three loose ranks.

Most of the boys, I noticed, were smiling. They were stealing glances at each other, exchanging smirks and even giggling. General Sir, with his oiled head and amazingly dirt-free boots glistening in the evening sun, was smiling too. Three adults who'd jumped down from the 4x4s stood next to the General to inspect this impromptu parade.

Two were young black guys dressed in khaki fatigues. The nearest had a cigarette in the corner of his mouth. The other, beyond him, was quite fat. His shirt buttons were so taut it looked ready to pop. I realised I hadn't seen a fat person in ages.

Odd as that was, it was the third guy who shocked me most. He was white and middle-aged with a firm jaw and an upright military bearing. Though I'd only ever seen his image on a screen before, I recognised him instantly. This was the man whose face I'd seen on General Sir's laptop, and also Mum's.

The sight of this man made my skin prickle. He hadn't looked my way yet but it was as if an electric current was already running through me. This guy had cropped up on Mum's laptop first, then General Sir's, and now he was here in person. Who the hell was he and what did he want?

It soon became obvious. He and the other adults began looking over the rag-tag rank before them. Among the troop of boys, the jokey atmosphere had faded, replaced with shifting uncertainty. They realised they were being judged, and in some cases rejected.

We watched as the fat guy and his friend with the cigarette walked up and down in front of the kids looking them over, poking them, manhandling them generally. The fat guy was the worst. He yanked one little kid out of line by the wrist, lifted up the boy's skinny arm and laughed in his face. Then he pushed him back into place so hard the kid tripped over and landed on his bum in the dirt. Cue more laughter.

General Sir let this happen without objecting. In fact, he smiled at the men's hilarity. All the while he was talking to the white guy, flicking his little baton in the direction of the kids for sale, talking up their value, or so it seemed.

The white man appeared unmoved. I couldn't see his

face in full, but in profile it looked stony. He had a stillness about him. No matter what General Sir said to him, he wasn't about to react.

The men in uniform were now separating the boys into two groups, those they wanted and those – such as the skinny little kid the fat one had pushed over – that hadn't made the cut. Those in the latter group looked crestfallen.

'The irony is too much,' Amelia whispered. 'From the look of it these men are selecting fighters for actual war, in which those boys could easily be killed. Staying here, though boring, is the comparatively safe option. Yet that lot there, the rejects, look miserable, while those off to face the real danger seem delighted.'

It was true; as the selection drew to an end the five boys who'd been successful were grinning at one another again. That wiry teenager there, in mismatched, broken shoes, now had a ticket out of here and was thumping his fist into his palm with a 'let's do this!' look on his face.

Amelia was right about the irony of the situation, but unlike her I sympathised with the whole success-over-failure thing: it doesn't really matter what the competition is, if I've entered into it, I want to win. The flip side of that is that losing hurts.

Mo put it more accurately. 'It's the way soldiers are trained the world over,' he murmured to Amelia. 'The most important step is making them *want* to fight. A soldier, once he's had his training, should feel it's his duty to use it in battle.'

General Sir, still joking with the white guy, had drifted

around to his other side, so that we were now standing in his line of sight. As he was motioning the man towards his quarters, he spotted us and grinned broadly. He beckoned us over with his arms held wide, shooting sidelong glances at the white guy, who'd swivelled to see us.

'And these are the new recruits I was telling you about,' General Sir was explaining. 'New recruits for my international brigade!'

I stared at the white man. He had a lean face, with a square brow and chin, and a level, unblinking gaze. His eyes were the colour of wet slate. He stood with his feet apart and his back straight, very still and upright, conveying the impression that standing, for him, meant taking a stand, rather than simply being in a particular spot.

Slowly he took in Mo, Amelia and Xander, and finally me. When our eyes met, the electricity connecting us surged like lightning. I swear he also flinched. He looked away immediately.

Who was this guy? How did he know General Sir? What did he want with kids from this camp? Why, simply by standing there, did he seem such a threat?

37.

General Sir waved us closer, his grin wider still. I didn't want to obey him but, smile or no smile, we had no choice. He said something I couldn't understand to the two goons who'd been picking out fighters, and then, in English, invited the white guy and the four of us into his quarters.

I didn't like the feel of this at all. In fact, I nearly bolted. Something about the way I was moving must have betrayed as much because Xander, always reassuring, put a hand on my shoulder as we stepped inside and whispered, 'Steady, Jack.'

Once we were inside, the General made a great show of offering everyone a cold drink from his stupid mini-fridge. It was full of Cokes this time. Where he got them from, I've no idea.

While he fussed about retrieving the drinks, I took a careful look around the little room. It was spick and span again, with the bed made and the laptop set precisely in the middle of General Sir's little table. The one door into the shack was to the left of that table. A big padlock lay on a shelf just inside the door. I'd seen it before: the General used it to lock up when he wasn't in the hut. The shack was actually quite sturdy, made of shiplap wood. It was gloomy. The only natural light fell into it through the open door, the shack having no windows.

General Sir didn't so much offer us kids a drink as hand us each a can. Amelia cracked hers open immediately. When he held one out to the white guy, however, he rejected it with an almost imperceptible shake of his head, keeping both hands behind his back as he stood there, upright, imposing and dismissive.

The fact that he was turning down the General's hospitality made me not want to accept it either, particularly not in front of this guy, but I was already holding the cold can in my hand, so I simply opted not to open it. I slid both hands behind my back instead and stood up as straight as the man in front of me.

'Yes, yes,' General Sir was saying. 'As I explained, this is my international contingent, supervised by little Mo here. A new project. Very entertaining! Also, a valuable asset,' he said under his breath. To us he said, 'This is Mr Leopold. Or Mr Leopard, as we say! He's an important man. I think you might be of interest to him.'

I wasn't sure how I felt about the 'supervised by Mo' bit, but now wasn't the time to argue. I kept my eyes on this Leopard guy. Having inspected Mo, his level gaze drifted from Amelia to Xander, missing me out.

'What are your names?' he asked them.

General Sir answered before any of us did. 'That's Xander, he's Jack, and this one is Melia.'

Amelia corrected him instantly: 'Amelia.'

The Leopard nodded, noting her objection and dismissing it at the same time. 'Amelia, Xander, Jack,' he said, but again, though he looked at my friends as he said their names, his eyes slid over me without apparently seeing me. He turned back to the General, a nonplussed look on his face.

'What use are they to me?' he said.

'You're not curious about them? How they came to be here; who might be missing them; where they're from?'

General Sir saying this brought Mum – poor Mum – to mind, and I had to hold myself back from flinging the Coke can, which I was still gripping tightly in my right hand, at his shiny little head.

'Why should I be?' said the Leopard.

'As well as the excellent, hand-picked, highly trained fighting force you came for,' General Sir went on, smooth as a used car salesman, 'maybe you would like to make me an offer for these . . . valuable specimens.'

The Leopard shrugged, as if to say: I doubt it.

'When I say valuable, I mean it,' General Sir insisted, a tetchy note in his voice. Clearly, he was annoyed by the Leopard's lack of interest. Like any good salesman – by which I mean exactly like those cringeworthy contestants on *The Apprentice* – he pushed on regardless. 'In the right hands, using the right channels, a person could make a small fortune. These are very valuable goods indeed.'

'Excuse me!' said Amelia, unable to keep her indignation

to herself. 'Goods?! We're people, not things. And we're right here listening!'

She had a point, but it backfired. General Sir, already frustrated by the Leopard's stony refusal to bite on his offer, decided to try another tack. He said something to Mo and followed up with, 'All of you, wait outside. Important negotiations must not be interrupted!'

Mo immediately did as he was told. We traipsed out, me last. The Leopard didn't so much as glance our way. He kept his eyes on General Sir, a withering look of near boredom on his face.

I had an urge to shout something – anything – to get his attention. I've no real idea why. What did his indifference matter to me? Either way, I held back, but once we got outside and I realised Mo was intending to head all the way back to the tent, I drew everyone up short.

'Let's stick around, see what happens,' I said.

'I'm not sure that's wise,' said Xander.

He's generally good at avoiding needless trouble, but I ignored him today. 'To plan an escape, we need to know as much of what goes on here as possible,' I whispered, trying to believe what I was saying and failing: it sounded so lame.

One of General Sir's bloodhounds was curled in the dirt beneath a nearby tree. I went over to it. The dog opened an eye and raised its lip above a yellow incisor as I approached, but there was no venom in the display and I heard no growl. When I bent to scratch the dog between the ears, I was ready to jerk back if it snapped at me, but it didn't. In fact, though its lip stayed half curled, the dog pushed its dusty head up against my hand, clearly enjoying the attention despite itself. I knelt there, gently working the fur on the back of the dog's neck, one eye on General Sir's quarters.

We were close enough to hear voices coming from inside. Or rather one voice: General Sir's. He got louder and louder, as if arguing with himself.

I strained to hear the Leopard's responses but couldn't. His stillness seemed to radiate from the shack. Elsewhere, there was movement. The kids who'd not been selected to fight slunk away while those who were off to war, all smiles, climbed into the waiting Land Rovers, ushered inside by the Leopard's goons.

That made sense. What surprised me, however, was that as soon as General Sir's voice became audible outside his shack, two kids with guns had materialised. One, Kayd, came out from behind the building itself, the other casually wandered into the clearing from the direction of the tents.

The door to General Sir's quarters banged open hard, kicked from within. The General himself emerged. He had a pistol in his hand, and even from this distance I could see the whites of his eyes.

Both boys with rifles went immediately to General Sir's side. The metallic click of gun mechanisms cocking cut through the hubbub. General Sir was waving the pistol in the direction of the door he'd just walked through. Sure enough, the Leopard emerged from the shack.

Whatever the shape of the row between the two men, the Leopard had remained calm while General Sir had lost his temper. The boy-enforcers weren't exactly aiming their guns at the Leopard, but they were resting them on their hips, muzzles pointing in his direction.

If he noticed this, he didn't show it, just strolled slowly past the little group as if he was taking a walk in the park. He caught nobody's eye: didn't look at us or even General Sir, just calmly crossed the clearing, heading for the Land Rovers.

'It was a good offer, a valuable opportunity, and you know it!' General Sir shouted after him.

The Leopard's pace neither quickened nor slowed.

'This disrespect, it's very bad for business!' General Sir hollered.

The Leopard climbed into his seat and closed the door.

'You'll be back,' shouted General Sir. 'You will. You're interested. We both know it!'

The Leopard's Land Rover did not take off in a cloud of dust. Instead it made a slow three-point turn and came to a halt next to General Sir and his enforcers. The second SUV fell in line behind the first. From where we were standing the sun, glancing off the Land Rover's windows, made it hard to see what was happening.

I couldn't see the Leopard at all. But he definitely held out a small package to General Sir, and General Sir, his shiny head still pulsing with rage, snatched it from him angrily. Without pausing, General Sir marched back to his shack as the two Land Rovers, carrying their cargo of fresh child soldiers, eased away down the track.

38.

'What was all that about?' asked Xander.

'It's pretty obvious,' said Amelia. 'Those guys were here to buy fighters from the General.'

'Have you seen them here before?' Xander asked Mo.

Mo shook his head. 'They are not General Sir's usual customers.'

'Who do they work for?' Xander asked. 'Where are those poor kids going to fight?'

'Government forces,' said Mo. 'Either they go north to Mogadishu, or further south to the border.'

'That Leopard guy didn't look much like a Somali government official,' said Xander. 'But I suppose there's no telling.'

Mo shrugged. 'He's a mercenary working with them, I think, to put distance between General Sir's black-market child soldiers and the officials. But the other two men wore Somali army uniform, that's how I know. Mercenaries fight on all sides. Often they have military experience in foreign armies. They sell their expertise to the highest bidder.'

'He sounded British to me,' I said. 'And he looked pretty together. General Sir's a nasty nut-job, but what he does makes a sort of sense. This is his conflict. Imagine coming here on purpose as a mercenary, just to make money out of the war, buying *children* to fight in it. That Leopard guy is just . . . beyond evil.'

'Yeah, but what was the row about?' asked Xander.

Mo, eyes to the ground, said, 'I think General Sir was trying to sell you to the Leopard as well,' he said. 'With his contacts he could ransom you on for even more money. But the Leopard wouldn't bite.'

'And the implications of that are pretty interesting,' said Amelia, as if explaining a bit of schoolwork, not theorising about our fate. 'Things can't be going too well from General Sir's perspective if he wants to pass us on to some random mercenary. Either he's not been able to make contact with our parents or they're not willing to pay for our release. Given that he appears to have a computer and adequate communications in place, the latter is the more logical, if surprising, conclusion.'

We sat in silence as her words sank in.

Amelia's reasoning sounded, as usual, correct. I'm not sure what the others were thinking about that, but I was torn. On the one hand, I have to admit it hurt a bit to imagine that Mum – and Amelia's and Xander's parents – weren't prepared to pay for our release, but on the other I was proud of them: led by Mum – and me – they were doing the right thing by holding firm. It was exactly what I'd asked her to do.

'If General Sir starts thinking we're not so valuable as hostages . . .' Xander began, but trailed off.

'He might put us to some other use,' said Amelia.

'Like what?' Xander asked.

Unable to stop herself, but clearly frightened by her own thinking, Amelia whispered, 'Since this is a training camp for child soldiers, the obvious answer would be to train us up. He may decide we'll sell for more as . . . cannon fodder.'

Nobody said anything as the implications of this sank in. Imagine actually fighting a war. Against other child soldiers and men. Being sniped at, machine-gunned, bombed. My tongue was running around the inside of my mouth, probing a painful cut inside my cheek. It felt raw, like an abscess. Bad food, without enough vitamins, can give you those; I'd read about that in a book on pirates, ironically enough. Not the modern type who'd kidnapped us; the old-school ones with eye-patches and parrots. At sea for months on end without sight of a vegetable or any fruit. Scurvy is a thing. Never mind being torn apart on a battlefield, we were already falling apart here. Anger welled up within me.

'It changes nothing,' I said. 'We got ourselves into this mess and we're going to get ourselves out of it. If anything, it just means we should put an escape plan into action sooner rather than later.'

Mo hung his head.

Xander said, 'Sure.'

And Amelia said, 'Of course.'

Through gritted teeth I muttered, 'I mean it.'

39.

Maybe it had to do with his disappointment at not having offloaded us on the Leopard, or possibly he'd been planning this visit all along: either way, General Sir pulled a chair into our midst after nightfall that evening and said, 'You know I have an English passport, like you guys?'

'Sure,' I said under my breath.

'I do. I lived there for a while. In London. A place called Camden.'

'That explains the accent,' said Amelia. 'But if you lived there, what are you doing here?'

'This is where I'm from originally.'

Despite myself I was interested. 'So, what happened?' I asked.

'My family were from Mogadishu. The capital. We endured the war at its worst here, during the 1990s. My father fought in it. He was killed when I was six.'

'That's a shame,' said Amelia. She's so unintentionally deadpan that even I, in that moment, couldn't work out whether she was being sarcastic or genuine.

'Sad, yes,' said General Sir, taking no apparent offence. 'What took you to England?'

'I went as a refugee. When my father was killed my mother fled with me and my brothers and sisters. To Ethiopia first. And from there a long and dangerous journey to England. My youngest sister died on the way. She was only a baby.'

'Also sad,' said Amelia.

In the pause that followed, something shrieked in the dark. It sounded panic-stricken and human. I thought of the boys held in the pits. They were still out there. General Sir took this opportunity to say, 'Noises always seem more sinister at night.' Whatever he intended by this comment, it wasn't reassuring.

'What *was* that?' said Xander.

'A wild dog, I think. They make a lot of noise but they're no real threat to us here.' He went on. 'I made it to England with my mother and two elder brothers, in the end.'

'My cousin lives near Camden,' said Amelia. 'I've been there loads. Why did you come back here? Didn't you like it?'

'My family liked Camden very much. We went to school and lived in a good house. My elder brothers still live in London. So does my mother. My brothers worked hard and they have done well. One has his own computer business now, and the other is a hospital physio. He helps . . . rehabituate people who've had accidents.'

'Rehabilitate,' said Amelia, unable to let the slip pass.

General Sir ignored her. 'I liked being in London, but other people,' he said vaguely, 'didn't like me being there

196

so much. There was a misunderstanding.' He smiled at us in turn. 'About a burglary, I think. Yes, a burglary. Teenage foolishness on my part.' He held up his hands and smiled harder.

I used to have nightmares about strangers coming into my room while I was asleep. Even locking the window didn't stop the bad dreams. I knew my fear was irrational: Mum told me all about the statistical improbability of a burglar targeting our house. But when I was about eight the nightmares got so bad, I refused to go to bed. Mum couldn't persuade me to and I even refused to go when ordered by Dad. I only went when my brother, Mark, offered to sleep on the floor in my bedroom, as a first line of defence. He kept it up for a week. Now, listening to General Sir casually admit to burglary, the thought crossed my mind that he'd been among the people I'd been so terrified of back home as a little kid.

'You left London because of a burglary?' I said.

He nodded and smiled. 'It was most regrettable.'

I looked at Mo. He stared back at me; it felt like he was willing me not to ask for more details. Since General Sir seemed to want the chance to elaborate, I held my tongue. I didn't want to give the maniac the satisfaction.

He sat back in his chair. 'So, yes, with my mother's blessing, I returned to our wonderful capital, Mogadishu. And from there –' he waved in the general direction of the darkness – 'my adventures brought me to this lovely part of the world!'

As if on cue, the wild dog noise started up again then,

closer than before, a series of overlapping yelps, each more shriek-like than the last. The sound wasn't so much menacing as deranged: the dogs seemed to be whipping each other up into a frenzy. Had they caught something? Were they killing it, or arguing over the spoils? I didn't know. As abruptly as the cacophony started, it stopped. In the silence that followed a shiver ran through me, all the way from my head to my toes.

General Sir knew we were terrified – of him, the camp, and the wild world beyond it. His work done, he simply rose from his chair, said, 'Sleep well!' and drifted off into the darkness.

'You too!' Xander called after him.

As ever he knew exactly how to defuse the moment. Though trembling, I couldn't help laughing. 'Great guy,' I said.

'Real charmer.'

Ignoring us, Amelia asked Mo outright, 'What really happened?'

'What he said, more or less.'

'It's the "more" bit I'm interested in.'

'The General broke many laws in London. For gangs and drugs mostly. He was young and often in trouble, doing bad things. Motorcycle robberies, even burglaries as he said. Being small and a good climber meant he could get in through upstairs windows. And for him there was never a minimum age for violence.'

'But why, specifically, did he flee London?' Amelia asked.

'There was a murder. General Sir was fifteen. A dispute

over drugs and territories. He killed another boy with a knife. But the police arrested someone else. They thought they had the perpetrator. Later they realised they were wrong. In the time gap General Sir's mother, thinking that the situation in Somalia was improving, put him on a plane to her sister in Mogadishu.'

'So he returned to the capital. How did he end up here, in the middle of nowhere?'

'He was recruited to fight in the conflict himself, and he immediately saw that children were valuable in war because so many children fought on both sides. They do what adults tell them; it doesn't matter if it's evil or good. But there are never enough children to fight the adults' wars! General Sir saw this. He spotted a business opportunity. He would find children by whatever means, teach them to be useful, and sell them to the highest bidder. According to camp rumour, he's been doing it ever since.'

40.

The wild dog noise made it hard to sleep that night. The following morning, bleary and exhausted and because there were no real toilets to use in camp, I took myself off to do my business a little way into the bush. As I was walking back, I heard another animal whimpering. The pitiful noise was intercut with a whacking sound.

Instinctively I went towards the noise and came upon Kayd. His back was to me and he had a stick in his raised hand. As I watched he brought it down on a small boy curled tight on the ground. Realising Kayd was laying into a child, I ran straight in yelling at him to stop.

Kayd ignored me. He didn't even look my way. He just brought the stick down hard again on the curled-up boy's back. Weirdly, the little boy didn't yelp at the blow. He just kept on with his whimpering. As Kayd lifted the stick again I closed in on him and grabbed it.

Kayd spun around. His eyes were blank, his lips expressionless. With his free hand he punched me hard in the chest. It would have been enough to knock me over if I hadn't been hanging on to the stick. As it was, I staggered backwards with all my weight, yanking at the stick as viciously as I could – hard enough, at any rate to rip it from him.

Kayd just stared at, or rather through, me. He didn't try to grab the stick back, or run at me, or yell. He looked almost bored. To have punched me one minute and be content simply to stare at me the next made little sense. Neither did the fact the small kid was still curled on the ground rather than running for cover.

I have to admit, I was fired up. I was so frustrated and frightened, and his face was so impassive it looked like a sculpture. I wanted to smash it to pieces.

I swung the stick at his face with all my might. I wanted to burst it open like a piñata. Every birthday party I ever went to in junior school had one of those stupid things. And I was always pretty good at destroying them. You just have to swivel from the hips, put your weight behind the blow, lean in.

The stick stopped in mid-air. I was swinging so hard the dead halt jerked me backwards. I turned in shock to see Mo. I had no idea where he'd come from but he'd arrived in time to catch the stick and he wasn't about to let it go. Everything about him said: 'No!'

In stopping me from hitting Kayd he was clearly trying to save me from myself. Still, I didn't like it. For a nanosecond I thought of ripping the stick free again, but instead I let it go.

Instantly Mo's expression changed. He laughed, slapped me on the shoulder, and tossed the stick back to Kayd, who caught it. Mo then said something, and although I had no idea what it was, I could tell from the tone of his voice he was making light of what had just happened. I've seen the same sort of thing often enough at school. An argument flares up and is about to go off properly, then somebody backs down pretending the whole thing is a joke. It's a way of saving face. Cowards use it. I didn't like that Mo had chosen this tactic for me, not one bit.

But we weren't in school. We were in a camp that turned slave children into child soldiers. The tactic may have been the same, but the consequences of not deploying it here were unknowable.

Kayd was staring right through me again, ignoring Mo's nothing-to-see-here joking entirely. I couldn't help but stare back. His eyes were a very dark brown but facing the morning sun they swam with tiny flecks of amber. Very slowly, he turned from me to the kid on the ground.

The little boy was still curled tight, shielding his head and neck with his hands. They were thin, with slight fingers. Why, oh why, hadn't he crawled off when he had the chance? Kayd was toying with the stick, daring me to challenge him for it again. It took every ounce of my willpower to stop myself. But Mo's forced jocularity was if anything more effective than his panic had been.

I had no choice but to trust him. I'm ashamed of it, but I stayed rooted to the spot as Kayd brought the stick down on the little kid's back one last lazy time. The boy's whimpering started up again. Kayd tossed the stick down next to him and walked off slowly towards General Sir's shack without looking back at us.

41.

As soon as Kayd had gone, Mo switched his attention to the little boy on the ground. During the beating his shorts had twisted round his waist so that the fastener was on his hip. He wriggled them back into place. He wasn't crying. Kayd must have hit him a dozen times with that stick, but the boy put up with the hurt as if it had been nothing more than a slap. Mo said something to him that actually made him smile, nod, and jog off towards the main camp. I couldn't believe a boy that young could shrug off such brutality.

'Compared to what's coming for him, that was nothing. It's almost helpful, in a way. Means he'll be less scared when he sees war.'

Mo wasn't defending Kayd so much as stating a fact. I thought of the kids I'd seen working the tantalum mine in the Congo, and the two General Sir had imprisoned in holes in the ground, and the dozens of little ones here being groomed to fight, and I thought of Mum and what she would want to do about it.

'When we escape, we're taking him with us,' I told Mo.

'Sure. Why not,' he said.

'I'm serious. In fact, any kid who wants out of here should be free to come too. A rebellion is what's needed. The more the better. With enough of us working together, the General will be powerless.'

Mo sighed. 'You've just seen Kayd at work. There are others loyal to General Sir who will stop us.'

'They'll try,' I said. 'But –'

'And even if we get past them, which we won't, there's the dogs. I've already told you about them.'

An idea came to me, obvious and yet surprising: 'Then we'll take the dogs with us as well.'

'What?' Mo looked at me like I was an idiot.

'They can't track us for the General if they're already with us, can they?'

'They're hunting dogs! They belong to him. What makes you think they'll come with us?'

'I've seen the way he treats them.' I shrugged. 'They're frightened of him, sure. That can make a dog obedient, but it doesn't make it loyal. There's a big difference.'

Mo sighed. 'Either the dog wants to do something or thinks it has to: the pain you'll feel when its teeth sink into your leg will be much the same.'

We'd been walking back to the others as we talked and now arrived at the tent. Xander and Amelia were sitting in front of it on plastic chairs. Mo and I sat down too, just as one of the little boys arrived with our breakfast. We each took a bowl from him. The sun was still low, bathing everything in a welcoming early morning light. Zoom in on the tent and chairs, cutting out the context, and we could have been on a camping holiday, about to tuck into some cornflakes. But we weren't in a campsite, with cereal, bowls and spoons. Breakfast here was more slop, eaten with our fingers. I ate it anyway and, between mouthfuls, told Xander and Amelia what I'd witnessed.

'Poor kid,' said Amelia. 'At least he wasn't badly hurt.'

'That's not the point,' I said.

'I reckon it was for him,' she countered.

'There are divisions here to exploit.'

'There are big kids terrorising little ones,' said Amelia. 'We can't do a lot to help them.'

Xander said, 'I think I see what Jack is getting at. The younger boys and girls could be helpful to us. At the moment they do what they're told because General Sir has a bunch of thugs working for him. It's too much to expect the little ones to rebel on their own. But with a leader to follow they might turn against General Sir. And with the dogs out of the equation he couldn't do much against a mass breakout.'

Mo had his head in his hands. Now he leaned back in his chair and spoke to the sky. 'You think they'll listen to you, get behind you, support you when you go up against Kayd and the enforcers, who have weapons to make their point with? You've got, what? Fists against their guns? Sticks at best. And you think you're their great hope?'

'No,' I said quietly. 'I'm not the great hope here. You are.'

Mo didn't reply to that. He set down his breakfast bowl, stood up and said, 'We need to start work,' instead.

42.

Over the next few days Amelia, Xander and I made plans. Despite himself, Mo was a part of them. He was working, eating and sleeping alongside us, so he didn't really have a choice but to overhear us, and I deliberately made sure he was in earshot.

To begin with he just listened, occasionally shaking his head in weary disbelief, even puffing out his cheeks from time to time, as if to say 'impossible' without words. But as the shape of what we were plotting became clear, with the difficulties we'd face along the way becoming more obvious at each step, he started making suggestions. I'd gambled on this, his hardwired resourcefulness. It was in his DNA: faced with a problem, Mo couldn't help trying to come up with a solution.

'How are we going to handle the dogs then?' Xander asked as we worked together to prise up a particularly reluctant stump.

'I've already started,' I replied, 'by trying to gain their

trust. I read a lot about dog training when we got Chester. Dogs read how you are around them. They're all about body language. Project calm and confidence and a dog will pick up on it.'

Amelia, who was levering a crowbar under the stump's tap root, now pulled it out, leaned on it, and said, 'Sure, body language is a big thing for canines, as it is for all animals in fact, but in my experience, dogs are more about treats.'

'We could save some of our food to feed to them,' Xander suggested.

'It would be a start,' Amelia replied. 'But I doubt they'd be much more impressed by that slop than we are. What we need and don't have is meat.'

'We could do with some of that ourselves,' said Xander. 'To help get our strength up.' He jabbed at the stump listlessly with his shovel. 'I've never felt so weak.' He looked it. Despite us having been outside more or less constantly, working in the sun, his dark skin was tinged a sallow grey. 'We're not exactly going to stumble over a pack of sausages out here though, are we?'

Mo had been hacking back some scrub a little way off. He stopped now and said, 'Not sausages, no.'

'Sounds like there's a but,' said Amelia.

'There are animals in the bush. You've heard the noises at night.'

'We're hardly equipped to bag an antelope though,' I said.

'There are ways of hunting for smaller prey. Fringe-tailed gerbils, acacia rats, Greenwood's shrews, and so on. Boys in the camp have done it before. I've seen them. Using snares.'

I thought of the snares I'd seen in the rainforest in the Congo, set by poachers. They were horrible things, as likely to harm an endangered species as anything else. Was it wrong of me to allow Mo to teach us how to set them here? No, I decided. First, we weren't in a national park or conservation area. And second, we were desperate. When I brought that up Amelia immediately suggested that the poachers had probably been desperate too, but I shut that thought out and set to learning from Mo.

He was a methodical teacher. We'd all learn how to build the snares, he said. That way we could make many between us. To start with he told us each to fetch the component parts: a stout forked stick (the sort that might make a good catapult, but bigger); three similarly strong straight sticks; and two lengths of string or twine, one thick, the other thin. That was it. Xander came up trumps on the string front with a discarded guy rope that we cut up using a sharp stone. For the thin string we butchered some shoelaces.

Once we had all the bits, we began by hammering the catapult stick, arms up, firmly into the ground. Then Mo showed us how to make a spring using one of the bits of string, wound round the 'Y' of the catapult and twisted tight with one of the long straight shafts.

It was ingenious: by delicately wedging the long arm against another of the straight sticks, which we'd also hammered into the ground, we created a spring-loaded arm on a hair trigger.

With the final component – the length of thinner shoelace – we made a noose which we attached to the sprung arm of the trap. The open 'O' of the noose went on the ground over the hair trigger, on top of which, Mo explained, we'd put the bait. Simple, but effective.

Once we'd got the materials together, making those first snares took less than half an hour. And over the next couple of days we scavenged more materials with which to make a few more.

Bait was the last ingredient. Mo suggested we use dollops of the very mush General Sir fed the rest of us for this purpose. Hearing that's what we'd be tempting our prey with, I rolled my eyes.

'You're sure they'll fall for that stuff?'

'It may not be your favourite but for a rat or gerbil it's rich . . . what do you call it?' Mo said.

'Pickings?' said Xander.

'In nutrients?' said Amelia at the same time.

'I was going to say "reward", but what you suggest is fine.'

Mo never revelled in it, but he was indispensable on so many fronts. I could come up with ideas, such as bribing the enforcers, but Mo knew who would stay loyal to General Sir no matter what and he obviously had the words with which to bribe those he thought might give in to temptation. Even determining which kids we could persuade to make a run for it would have been impossible without him.

When we weren't working, and whenever General Sir and his henchmen were out of sight, we set traps both near the field in which we were put to work, and in the bush nearer General Sir's camp. Mo helped us choose the spots. Mostly these were little funnel-shaped clearings, or channels between clumps of scrub, anywhere a small animal might come upon the bait and take it.

And when we were safely in camp, Mo increasingly split his time between our little area and the bigger tent enclave housing the real child-soldiers-to-be, where, head bowed among a little group or sitting on a log with a child, he had what he described as 'quiet conversations'.

The exact topic of these was anyone's guess. We were powerless to do anything but wait for him to report back, and this he did without specifics. 'I'm working on it,' he might say. Or, 'Softly, softly; patience is a virtue, yes?' Mostly he'd answer, 'Don't worry, I'll tell you when I have news.'

I found this vagueness unsettling, and in private I asked the others whether we should pressure Mo to give us more detail. Amelia, ever logical, pointed out that we had little to pressure him with: without him we were lost. That didn't help much, but Xander said Mo's quiet approach made sense to him for now. So I sat on my misgivings and waited.

43.

The morning after we'd set the first snares, I crept out of the tent early and went to inspect them. They hadn't worked. Worse than that, two of the five we'd built had gone off without trapping anything. The gunk-bait in them was gone, and something had gnawed through one of the lengths of string, but the snare was empty. I bit my tongue, retied the noose, set the trap again. I didn't want to break this disappointing news to the others, but they were up when I returned and Amelia quickly put two and two together.

'Empty-handed,' she said.

'Did you check them all?' asked Xander.

Amelia answered for me. 'Of course he did.'

Xander's face fell.

Mo cut in gently with, 'What were you expecting?'

'Well, something, I suppose,' Xander replied. 'Not nothing.'

I hadn't even told them about the snares that had gone off unsuccessfully and decided not to now. Somehow Xander's bitter disappointment was my fault. 'It's early days,' was the best I could muster.

'Indeed it is,' said Mo more brightly. 'Just one night! Trust me, the snares will work if we give them time. And today we can make a few more to increase the probability of success.'

I tried to look as positive as he sounded for the benefit of the others, but I didn't like the idea that we had to rely upon him to boost our morale. What, practically, could I do to help us? The traps needed re-baiting. When our breakfast slop arrived, I saved a pinch of mine in a folded leaf. I tried to do this surreptitiously, waiting for a moment when the others were distracted by a squabble that had broken out between two of the little kids, whose fight over one of the wooden guns (at least it wasn't a real one) had spilled across the dirt patch separating the main clutch of tents from ours, but Mo saw me do it.

'I'll come with you, help check everything works again,' he said.

'If you like, but I think I know what I'm doing.'

'You're disappointed,' said Mo. 'In fact, it's a good sign.'

'What is?'

'If something disturbed the traps, took the bait, it means we nearly succeeded.'

'It would be a better sign if the snare actually worked, surely.'

'Of course,' said Mo. 'But still.'

He followed me out of camp. The flies were up already – it was a still morning – but I'd learned to wave them away more lazily, which somehow stopped them being quite so maddening. I went straight to the first trap that needed re-baiting. Mo watched me do it and I was relieved that he said nothing; I didn't need his supervision after all.

The short walk to the other spent snare took us past one that had been undisturbed just an hour ago. As we approached it Mo suddenly shot forward, running low to the ground.

He'd spotted a movement. Unbelievably, something was caught in the snare, and Mo was immediately upon the little creature, smothering it with both hands.

He had his back to me. I barely had a chance to feel sorry for whatever it was – at least it hadn't been struggling against the noose for long – before he'd dispatched it with a sharp flick of his wrist. By the time I'd caught him up he'd removed the noose and was holding the creature, limp now, in an outstretched hand. It looked like a big gerbil.

'Here!' he said, offering it to me.

I've said before that I'm no fan of rodents, and to be honest the last thing I wanted to do was take the dead gerbil from Mo, but I was even less a fan of appearing squeamish before him. Also, I was genuinely delighted the snare had worked. We needed this result. The gerbil was warm to touch. Its head and tail flopped either side of my extended palm, opening up the fur on its neck. Sandy orange at the tips, the fur close to the animal's body was white. I didn't like the idea of the dead gerbil in my hand, but in that quiet moment its warmth and delicate beauty sent a strange feeling – a sort of triumphant sadness – right through me.

We checked the other traps and found them empty. But

that didn't matter now: we had proof of success. I'd trudged back to camp earlier, but the two of us had a spring in our step now.

Mo had noted who made the successful trap. He wasted no time in congratulating Xander with, 'Your snare worked!'

Xander's mouth fell open.

By way of proof, Mo pulled the dead gerbil from his shirt pocket and held it up for Xander to inspect.

'Huh! Look at that,' said Xander. 'I can't believe it.'

'Looks pretty incontrovertible to me,' Amelia said.

The hound I'd stroked was still sleeping on its side under the thorn bush. Another was nosing in the dirt a little way off. 'I say we give it to the dogs straight away,' I said.

'Won't they fight over it?' asked Xander.

'We'll give them a piece each,' said Mo, deadpan, pocketing the gerbil again.

'But we don't have a knife to cut it up with,' said Amelia.

'We don't need one,' Mo replied, standing up. In plain view he set off for General Sir's shack, but rather than approaching the front door he disappeared round the back of the little building. He was only out of sight for a minute. When he emerged, he was carrying the four tools we'd be using that day in our field-clearing: the spade and mattock under one arm, the crowbar and axe in the other.

'He's going to cut a mouse up with an axe?' Xander said under his breath as Mo approached.

Mo had good hearing. 'No,' he said, 'not the axe.' He set down everything but the spade and then in one fluid movement he fished out the gerbil, dropped it onto the dirt, placed the metal spade tip squarely across the little creature's midriff, and stamped hard on the spade's shoulder, cutting the gerbil in half.

I have to admit I flinched.

Amelia, however, just said, 'Fair enough, I suppose.'

'You're already friends with that one,' Mo said, pointing at the sandy-coloured dog I'd stroked. He bent to pick up one piece of the gerbil and offered it to me. 'You may as well be the one to feed him.'

The dismembered creature's golden fur was bloodstained. I held its back end by the tail, trying to look like I didn't mind. The others watched me. The dog appeared to be sleeping, but raised its head again before I got to it. Its black nose was twitching. As I arrived it levered itself upright, head still low.

Fearing the dog might snap at my hand, I nearly tossed the half-gerbil at its feet, but held back. As much as possible, the dog had to associate the food with me. I ran my fingers through its coarse fur and murmured nonsense to it, doing my best to project calm. This seemed to work. When I held my offering out the dog just nosed at it before taking it from me surprisingly delicately.

I stepped back. The dog, still holding the treat, eyed me suspiciously for a second, perhaps fearing some sort of trick. Was I about to grab it back? Not prepared to risk that, the dog slunk away. It obviously wanted to eat its prize alone, but the other hound had caught wind that something was up and trotted after it.

Thankfully Mo, thinking quickly, snatched up the

remaining lump of gerbil and intercepted the second dog with it. This one was thicker set, black and tan, with muscled shoulders and a broader head. It looked part Rottweiler.

I'm not sure whether Mo would have done what I did off his own bat, but he's nothing if not a quick learner and he too stroked the dog before feeding it. Unlike the thinner dog, this one gulped down the morsel quickly and immediately looked back up at Mo as if to say, 'Got any more?'

'We'll need to set more traps,' said Xander.

'Later,' said Amelia, nodding in the direction of General Sir as he emerged backwards from his quarters. He was holding the big silver padlock I'd spotted inside earlier, and now secured the door with it, snapping the lock into place. The thing about a padlock is, you can lock it without a key. Why was I thinking about that? I don't know. I was just pleased he hadn't seen us with the dogs. I somehow doubted he'd like us feeding them, even if he didn't work out why we wanted to do so.

'Why are you still here?' he called to us. 'You have work!' He pointed his stupid baton at us and flicked it in the direction of the clearing field. 'You can't do anything helpful with the tools here. Get going. Make yourselves useful!'

44.

Over the next few days we did what we could to ready ourselves for our escape. At night, top to toe in the tent, we planned, and during the days we prepared.

We set extra traps further afield and checked them in the grey light of before-dawn. Sometimes the little animals we caught – desert gerbils, grass rats mostly – were already dead, choked on the line, but mostly we had to dispatch them ourselves.

Mo showed me how to do this. You hold the poor creature by its back legs, run your other hand down to its neck, grip it behind the head, pull and twist.

I didn't like doing it, and Xander flatly refused, but Amelia had fewer qualms. Inspecting the traps with me early one morning she came upon by far our biggest catch, an oversized rabbit Mo later told us was a Cape hare. Immediately she saw it struggling she ran to put it out of its misery swiftly. I admit I winced at the crack I heard as she did it.

'What?' she asked. When I didn't answer she said, 'Just

because it's audible that doesn't change what's actually happening, namely the breaking of a spinal cord.'

'I suppose not,' I said.

We fed most of what we caught to the dogs immediately, there being no way of keeping meat out of the day's heat. On the plus side, the dogs cottoned on very quickly indeed. The hound I'd befriended even started following me around on my return each morning, looking hopeful.

After another benumbing day in the stump-field, Mo, who'd been out among the other kids, re-joined us in the tent. 'I have nine who'll come when I say,' he reported. 'And three of the five enforcers will accept a payment for turning a blind eye. The other two, Liban and Kayd, I cannot trust; they know nothing for now.'

'What sort of payment are we talking about?' asked Xander.

'Your sunglasses, for one.'

'They're cracked, but sure.'

'And from Amelia, your wristwatch.'

The watch was a chunky plastic diving model. Like Xander's sunglasses, Amelia had managed to hang on to it, and was equally prepared to give it up now.

'Whatever,' she said. 'That's two things. What's the third?'

'For Nabil, the eldest, something of more value.'

I knew what he was getting at: our diving treasure. We'd not mentioned the rings since Amelia revealed she'd hung on to them, but Mo, no fool, hadn't forgotten.

'What have you told him we've got?' asked Xander.

Quietly Mo said, 'I wasn't specific, just explained you have a little jewellery.'

'I'm surprised he's impressed by jewellery,' said Amelia.

'If it's gold it's more valuable here than currency,' Mo replied.

'When do we go then?' asked Xander, addressing the question more to Mo than me.

'When the time is right. We want to minimise the risk.'

I was grinding my teeth. 'The longer we leave it, the more of a risk we're taking. The little ones could give something away.'

'But we need to stockpile water, what little food we can spare or steal, and we need to neutralise General Sir, Liban and Kayd,' Amelia said, adding, 'as best we can, at least.'

'We've discussed that. There's no perfect moment,' I replied. 'The important thing is not to miss our chance entirely by waiting too long.'

The fact was, we couldn't make our move until Mo gave the go-ahead: without his say-so the little ones wouldn't come and the enforcers, even with bribes, wouldn't stand down. I was therefore relieved when he said, 'Jack's right, the sooner the better, I suppose.'

'The dogs are already onside, at least,' said Xander. 'When the snares next come up trumps, we should take that as a sign.'

'That makes no actual sense,' murmured Amelia. Then she surprised me by adding, 'But I know what you mean. Here,' she went on, taking off her watch. 'You might as well have this now, and this too.' From I don't know where, she'd already magicked up the smallest of the rings, a simple gold band that caught what little moonlight there was in the tent. She handed both over to Mo, saying, 'You too, Xander. Give him your glasses so he can buy off the boy guards. May as well sweeten them in advance.'

We talked on into the night, mostly about silly stuff – like what we'd eat when we had the chance to choose again (me: a cheeseburger and chips; Xander: fish pie; Amelia, weirdly specific: half an avocado filled with balsamic vinegar, followed by the other half; and Mo: a glass of cold milk). The thought of these things was delicious and a torment at the same time. Still, it was a diversion, just for a bit. Before long, with the others already asleep, I was back wondering when we could risk bolting. As it happened, a factor none of us had considered came into play sooner than I had imagined possible.

45.

That night I dreamed of Pete floundering in the distant wake of his dive boat, and of the man I called Dad for fourteen years turning his back on me, and – as ever – of my poor brother Mark dying on the pavement at my feet.

I sat bolt upright, blinking in the pitch dark. For a second I had no idea where I was. The tent was flapping hard. A gale had got up. The air tasted funny, burnt almost, charged with something. I assumed the others were still asleep beneath their blankets but it turned out Mo was awake and he somehow sensed I'd woken up.

'Wind storm,' he whispered. 'It will soon pass.'

In fact it didn't. The canvas was still whip-cracking when daybreak turned it grey. I got up ahead of the others and staggered outside. The wind wasn't actually as wild outside as it had sounded in the tent, but it was full of grit and smelled of fireworks.

Though I washed my face at the water butt I felt instantly grimy again as I set off with Mo to check the traps. The scrubland hissed and buzzed in the gloom. We walked the zigzag route between our snares in silence. I thought they'd all be empty, that the commotion of the wind would have driven all the foraging animals back to their burrows, but I was wrong. We'd set two new snares the day before, bringing our total to seventeen, and three of them – our biggest haul yet – had worked. The sky was a rushing purple bruise as we made our way back to camp. I put my head down against the wind-grit and trudged on, then felt Mo's hand on my arm.

'Look.'

Ahead of us, standing stock still between two thorn bushes, stood a huge goat-like animal. Its horns were scimitars, a metre long at least, as thick as my thigh at the base and dagger-sharp at the tip. The creature was so pale in the half-light it looked like a marble ghost, its stillness accentuated by the rushing wind.

We stared at it and it stared at us and the wind rose and fell and rose again and for what seemed an age nothing moved. At length the goat turned and picked its way through the bush.

'Ibex,' said Mo.

'It was huge!' I said. 'I've not seen one before.'

'Neither have I, not an albino.'

The ibex had radiated a calm that stayed with me as we trudged back to Amelia and Xander. It made me bury our snare-spoils rather than feed them to the dogs immediately.

Mo understood why. Neither of us said anything.

We went to work in the field as usual that day, attacked the stump roots as we always did, but although the wind raged the steadiness of the white ibex stayed with me. It helped me think clearly. The wind was tiring, but it could still be a good thing. Every time it dropped for a moment my spirits slumped, but happily the next gust always seemed harder than the last.

By the afternoon it was howling. Heading back to camp, filthy with the usual sweat and dirt, we were all coated in fine red dust as well. The stuff had got up my nose and into my ears and my hair was thick with it. But I didn't mind. Mo caught my eye and returned my smile.

Seeing this, Amelia said, 'This is worse than normal, and yet you're grinning about it. Why?'

Xander had cottoned on. He said, 'If the wind is like this tonight it could provide a diversion.'

'You're thinking we might go today!' she said. I couldn't quite tell whether the lightness in her voice was excitement or trepidation.

As calmly as I could I replied, 'Yes. We'll go tonight.'

46.

We arrived back in camp, ate our slop, and waited for the
sun to set. As it did one of the tents in the main area came
loose in a gust of wind so strong it also upturned some of
the plastic furniture. A group of boys struggled with the tent,
blown in on itself, in the gloom. General Sir was nowhere
to be seen. He had retreated to his quarters.

Under the guise of going to help the boys secure the tent,
Mo set off to prime those who'd be coming with us. Amelia,
Xander and I went to General Sir's.

His door was shut. I knocked on it and called to him,
lacing my voice with worry. 'General Sir. Amelia needs help.'

Before the door even opened Amelia doubled over between
Xander and me, holding her stomach.

'What is it?' General Sir asked, cracking the door an inch.

'Cramps,' Amelia said through gritted teeth. 'I get them
sometimes.'

'It's a girl thing,' added Xander.

This unnerved the General, but only momentarily. Looking

224

Amelia up and down he said, 'What do you expect me to do about it?'

'Painkillers,' Amelia hissed. Between impressive grimaces she went on: 'Without them I've ended up in hospital before now. I passed out and had a sort of fit. They thought I might swallow my tongue.'

'There is no hospital.'

'We know!' said Xander, sounding properly panicked. 'If she has painkillers she won't need to go! You must have some.' He risked putting a hand on the door as he said this and it worked – General Sir drew it open further.

'Oh God!' moaned Amelia, slumping to her knees on the threshold.

Xander and I heaved her forward into the room as General Sir stepped back. His laptop was open. A football match, of all things, was playing on it, complete with tinny commentary.

As we'd planned, Amelia toppled over entirely the moment we loosened our grip on her, flopping forward at the General's feet. She did a brilliant job of writhing around, clutching at herself. General Sir was completely distracted. Xander got between him and me for good measure, but he was transfixed by Amelia rolling around on the floor.

I snatched the padlock from the shelf inside the door and shoved it deep into my back pocket, undetected. General Sir came to his senses and fished a pack of pills out of the fridge.

'Here,' he said, handing it to her. 'We don't want you dying on us, I suppose.'

Amelia had clawed herself upright between us. Xander

propped up her elbow. To my surprise she took two of the pills immediately and pocketed the pack.

Xander pointed at the laptop and said, 'Good game?'

'Eh?' said General Sir, but his eyes darted back to the screen.

'Sorry to have disturbed you,' said Xander, though he was largely drowned out by another of Amelia's groans. 'We'll take her to lie down,' he went on. 'Let's hope the pills do the trick.' He nodded at the screen again. 'Have a good night.'

And with that we backed out of the room, still supporting Amelia between us. I had a hand on the door and pulled it firmly shut behind me as we retreated, holding my breath. If he saw the missing padlock straight away we were done for: he'd stop us in our tracks before we'd taken our first step. But he generally kept inside after dark, and in a windstorm like this he was even less likely to venture out until the morning.

By locking him in we'd buy ourselves extra time. Every minute counted. As Amelia spat the pills out in the dirt I quickly secured the padlock through the hasps on the outside of the door and locked it. Any click it made was blown away by the wind. The three of us exchanged a look of relief, then jogged back to our tent to rendezvous with Mo.

He was there already, crouched low on the blankets, wide-eyed with expectation. 'You succeeded?' he asked.

'He's locked in, yes, for now.'

'Watching a football match,' added Amelia. 'With the second half still to play.'

How she'd thought to notice that while doing her dying

dog routine I've no idea, but the thought comforted me: if General Sir was stuck into the match, it was even less likely he'd want to stretch his legs outside for now.

'They're all ready,' said Mo.

'With water?'

'Each has a bundle or pack with a full water container and even a little food.'

'And the bribes, did they work?'

'Oh yes,' he said. 'Better than I expected.' He looked at Amelia. 'Your ring in particular. I even managed to get us a little extra help with that.' A bashful smile spread across his face as he lifted a hem of the blanket at his feet. 'Check this out!'

A revolver lay in the blanket's folds. It was battered and ancient-looking, with a stubby black barrel that glimmered in the near dark. I picked it up. The thing was astonishingly heavy.

'It's Nabil's. General Sir keeps all the guns under lock and key after nightfall. But Nabil's had this one out for ages. We can use it on Kayd and Liban.'

'We have a plan to deal with them, and as far as I remember it doesn't involve us actually shooting anyone,' said Xander tentatively.

Amelia said. 'What's the catch?'

'It's a real gun but Nabil has no bullets for it. Still, he's not entirely sure Kayd and Liban know that.'

'Not entirely sure,' I murmured.

Xander, relieved we weren't about to murder anyone, now backed Mo up. 'It can only help, I suppose,' he said.

'Unless it makes us cocky, and Kayd and Liban *do* know it's out of ammo,' said Amelia.

She was right, of course, but to boost our morale I said, 'Fair point, we shouldn't get overconfident.' I took a deep breath. 'Let's get on with it!'

47.

Working swiftly in the gloom we dismantled our tent. Not to take with us, just so that we could harvest its guy ropes and poles. Though the wind yanked the tent around as we worked, the ropes untied easily enough. The plan had been to use the poles as weapons. They were heavy and sharp-tipped, after all. Now we had the handgun as well. I'd picked that up and shoved it in the waistband of my jeans without Mo objecting. Once we'd gathered what we wanted we set off through the gale for the main clearing.

The idea was that those who Mo had managed to bribe – Nabil and the others – would have made themselves scarce, leaving just Kayd and Liban in their tent. Heading that way, I felt my heartbeat pulsing in my neck. If they'd got wind something was up and were prepared for us we'd have a harder time overpowering them.

The wind was hammering so noisily we didn't need to tread softly, just jogged straight up to the tent. I wanted to pause, and if I had I bet the others would have hesitated too. But we'd been through the plan often enough and the adrenaline was pumping, so there was no point in stopping to gee ourselves up. With the gun in one hand and a tent pole in the other I speared straight in.

Their tent was bigger than ours. You could stand up in it. I'd half expected they'd be waiting for us, but they were stretched out in the gloom. Liban jumped to his feet as soon as we entered. I ran straight at him, knocked him back down and waved the gun in his face. He got the picture pretty quickly, raised his hands, said something that clearly meant, 'Don't shoot'.

Mo put a hand on my arm but I wasn't about to lower the gun. He started talking to Liban, his voice a persuasive blur in my ear. I shifted my attention to Kayd. He hadn't moved, not even to turn his head my way. It was unnerving. He looked dead. But of course he wasn't. He was just lying there pretending to be asleep, despite the noise.

I nodded at Xander, who edged closer to Kayd, holding his tent pole like a spear. Was he going to prod him awake with it? He never got the chance. I've no idea how Kayd, facing the other way, sensed Xander's approach, but as soon as the tip of Xander's spear edged within reach Kayd whipped round, grabbed it, and jerked Xander forward in one swift movement.

Caught unawares, Xander was too slow to brace himself. He staggered forward just as Kayd erupted from the ground with a roar. In an instant Kayd had Xander by the throat. The tent-pole spear was useless to Xander at such close quarters. He dropped it.

The two boys were a similar size to look at, but although Xander is no pushover he was no match for Kayd in strength. Xander was flailing at Kayd with one hand while trying to prise the boy's fingers from his neck with the other.

In the dusk they staggered wildly, the fabric of the tent snapping and cracking in the wind. I had to take control of the situation. I yelled, 'Stop,' quick-stepped towards Liban, and shoved the barrel of the pistol hard up under his chin. 'Stop! Or else!' I shouted at Kayd.

Either he didn't understand, knew the gun to be empty, or simply didn't care whether I shot Liban or not. Whatever the reason, he ignored me completely.

But he ignored everyone else – except Xander – as well. This meant he didn't spot Amelia as she sidestepped me, swinging her tent pole like a baseball bat. The crack of it hitting Kayd's skull cut through the wind-roar. His head jerked sideways with the blow and his knees buckled. I was amazed at Amelia's ferocity: she followed up the first blow with a second, just as savage. It knocked Kayd onto all fours. She would have smacked him again if Xander hadn't stepped between the two.

He hauled Kayd up onto his feet. The boy was in a daze but registered the gun now. I was pushing it so hard up under Liban's chin that the notched barrel seemed to have disappeared into his skin. I released him, spun him round, stuck the gun between his shoulder blades and marched him out of the tent.

'Let's go!' Xander hissed at Kayd.

He, Amelia and Mo drag-carried Kayd into the storm. The wind, still full of grit, whipped at us. The night sky was a moving mass, shredded clouds piling by, obscuring the stars and moonlight. Amelia had split Kayd's head. Blood glimmered on the side of his face and neck. I almost felt sorry for him. But given the chance he'd have done worse to any of us. Loyal to General Sir, he'd certainly stop us leaving if he could. I forced Liban on at a jog, heading for the pits.

48.

I braced myself for Liban and Kayd to fight back when they
cottoned on to where we were going, but it didn't happen.
We made it to the pits without either of them so much as
raising their heads. Still, would they resist when we ordered
them inside?

Mo had made that less likely by choosing this as the
rendezvous point for those kids whom he'd persuaded to
come with us. They stood like a welcoming committee
as we approached, spread out in a horseshoe around the
sunken cages.

There were five of these in total. Whether at Mo's
suggestion or on their own initiative, someone had already
pried up two of the metal cage doors. The group closed
around us as we arrived. Many hands funnelled the two
enforcers into the ground.

Nobody said anything. It felt like a silent ritual, turning
the tables on these bullies, putting them in their place.
Somebody had put a water bottle in each hole. Once they

were crouched inside Mo issued another order and two of the bigger helpers shut the cage doors.

Mo slid one of the long bolts into place. I immediately knelt to fasten the other. The bolt was stiff and crudely made, the metal rough. Still, it was inaccessible from inside, and way too strong to break. I ground it shut. We stood back. The wind boomed and groaned. It seemed louder now that it was near dark.

'Next step, the dogs,' I said. 'You dug up the snare-spoils?'

Mo nodded, reached inside his bag, and pulled out a piece of plastic in which he'd folded our most recent catches. He'd already cut them into pieces. I took a morsel. Xander did too.

Together with Mo and Amelia, we jogged back to where I'd last seen the dogs, sheltering in the lee of General Sir's shack. One of them – the one I'd befriended – was still there, a solid shape in the gloom. For a moment I was worried. What if we couldn't find the other one? But dogs are uncanny. At home, I swear Chester knows when I'm about to feed him before I do. He's always right there as I pick up his bowl to fill it.

Now, the dog, sensing our approach, was already up on its feet, and the other, thicker-set, dog must have sensed its expectation. It emerged from behind the water butt just as I was offering the bloodhound its treat.

Xander tossed his scrap at the bigger dog's feet. As it bent to snaffle it Amelia slipped a guy-rope noose under the dog's collar and fastened it with a clove-hitch knot. The other dog sat obediently, eyeing me for more to eat, while I did the same.

The ropes were just a precaution. If we had to pull the dogs away they'd come in handy. As it was, I reckoned both of them would have followed us anyway, especially after Mo had shown them both another sliver of bush meat. In a place where there wasn't much in the way of treats going, we'd made ourselves a source of something good, so they wanted to be with us. It was as simple as that. I let the hound's makeshift lead trail on the ground behind him as he followed us back to the pits. The thickset dog came too, led by Xander.

Perhaps because they wanted to distance themselves from Kayd and Liban in their cages, or simply because that's what he'd told them to do, Mo's band of escapees had already moved off into the near darkness. We caught up with them soon enough. With a brief, 'Everyone good to go?' to us and, I assume, the same question to the group in Somali, Mo set off.

There was no doubt who was in charge now. Mo led the way at a good pace. In single file, we picked our way purposefully through the scrub, heading south. My night vision had kicked in. Everything was shades of starlit grey and I could follow what path there was well enough.

The plan was to head for the border with Kenya. Mo reckoned it would be a two- or three-day hike, off-road. We couldn't risk being passed on a track or spotted in a village. Though there weren't that many settlements about, Mo insisted General Sir had eyes in all of them.

Our best chance lay in picking up a river ('more of a stream, really') Mo said lay some twenty-five kilometres away. It clipped the border near a settlement called Kolbio, which lay on the Kenyan side. We'd cross there.

By tracking the river upstream we'd know we were going in the right direction, and we'd have water when what we were carrying ran out. When Amelia had queried whether the General would guess at that plan Mo just shrugged. 'He may do, but more likely he'll think we go the quickest route, following the paved road. Or he might think we'd head for the sea.'

Either seemed a fair assumption. I ran through the discussion as we padded on in silence beneath the stars, feeling strong, optimistic even. So far, the plan was working. General Sir wouldn't realise we were actually gone until he'd shot his way out of his shack, hopefully in the morning. Kayd and Liban were stuck underground for the night with only the screaming wind for company, and General Sir's tracking dogs were literally eating out of our hands, for now. We had a little food, full water bottles, and we were all tough kids. Mo's band were actual trainee soldiers! If we put our heads down and just kept going, surely we'd make it.

Even as I thought all this, I knew in my gut I was wrong to be hopeful. I often get a sense when something's about to go wrong, and this was no exception. I just didn't realise how quickly it was going to happen.

49.

For the first hour or two it seemed we were making good progress. In single file, at a pace somewhere between a swift walk and a trot, we pushed on into the wind and dark.

Mo was at the front. He'd told one of the older boys, a broad-shouldered kid called Addie, to bring up the rear. The rest of us were strung out along the line.

I was near the back with one of the youngest of Mo's crew immediately in front of me. He had thin little legs made all the more scrawny-looking by the high-top trainers he was wearing. They had to be too big for him, surely.

I fixated on those shoes as they padded along in front of me. Despite their size, the boy seemed to glide along in them. I followed, matching his step where I could, since he read the rough ground so well.

We got into a rhythm. I zoned out, marvelling at how nimble that little kid was, concentrating on keeping up, conserving my strength as best I could, focusing on each individual footstep, and not allowing myself to think of the great distance ahead.

Nobody spoke, or at least I didn't hear anyone over the wind. We forged on until, out of nowhere, an abrupt grunt and a thumping noise came from behind me.

I turned to see Addie sprawled on the ground. Thinking quickly, I called out for the others to stop; if I hadn't, and they'd carried on, we could have been separated entirely. As it was my 'Stop!' reached Xander and he passed it on to the front of the line, prompting Mo and the others to double back.

We gathered around Addie. His pack had come off. I picked it up to give it back to him and realised it was at least double the weight of mine. He'd hurt his ankle as he fell. Mo squatted with him as he tested it. The boy winced putting weight on his left foot, but forced himself to take a few ginger steps.

'Not a good start,' Amelia pointed out.

'He'll shake it off, won't he, Mo?' Xander said hopefully.

Addie's face was concrete in the half-light, giving nothing away.

Mo asked him something. If he thought he could keep up, I assume. I sensed Mo weighing whether, for the good of the group, we should leave Addie there. Just as I was about to object and tell him we should give the boy a bit more time to walk off the sprain, I felt something tickly against my thigh. I thought it was the dog's tail brushing me, but when I looked down he was on my other side. Instinctively I slapped at my thigh, just as a sharp pain crackled across it. I'd made contact with something, knocking it off me, I thought.

'What's up?' asked Xander.

Something had bitten or stung me. I knew that. But I didn't know what it was. Though I inspected the ground I couldn't see anything, just greyed-out dirt, rocks and scrub.

'Nothing,' I said. 'A mosquito, possibly.'

'Which you're looking for on the ground?' said Amelia.

'Dumb, eh?' I admitted.

I knew it wasn't a mosquito. The thought of what it might have been filled me with dread: a scorpion; a spider; even, possibly, a snake? I had no idea! And I would never know. I couldn't do anything about whatever it was, except hope.

Addie had finished rubbing at his ankle. He was insisting he could go on. Meanwhile, the electric nip I'd felt had softened to an ominous pulsing sensation. Real fear gripped me then. Might the bite have been poisonous? Was the venom working its way into my bloodstream?

'You're sure you're all right, Jack?' said Xander.

'Fine, yes,' I replied.

But I wasn't. The throbbing grew heavier, giving me a dead leg from knee to hip. Addie was flexing his foot and Mo, who'd been focusing on him rather than me, had unscrewed the cap of his water bottle. Around us other kids did the same. If Amelia or Xander suspected I wasn't telling the truth they were too worried to press the point.

'Wait,' said Amelia.

Mo turned around.

I wasn't prepared for what she said next. 'Where's the other dog?'

The hound was still with us, sitting patiently beside me, but she was right, I'd not seen the heavier-set dog since we stopped.

Xander said, 'I'm sure he's around here somewhere,' without conviction.

'You had him tethered, didn't you?' said Amelia.

Xander didn't reply.

'If he's gone, it will be back to camp,' murmured Mo.

My pulsing leg was lead-heavy. A wave of helplessness swept through me, very nearly dropping me to my knees.

We were in the middle of nowhere, in the dead of night, with the sky howling above us, on the run from a crazy, slave-driving warlord. I'd been bitten or stung by God-knew-what. My leg was turning to stone; for all I knew the rest of me would follow and I'd seize up entirely. I might even die. On top of that, one of the tracker dogs we'd worked so hard to tease away from General Sir had slunk off back to him. If Mo was right about that then the dog would be able to follow its own trail here at the General's command, and before long they'd outrun us. The situation was completely hopeless.

'Talk about "you had one job",' said Amelia, acid in her voice.

Xander's head dropped.

I turned to Amelia. Truthful to a fault, she's never normally mean. To have snapped at Xander like that she had to be panicked to the point of an imminent meltdown. Such a loss of control – in her, particularly – was frightening.

Xander, never normally at a loss for words, was mute. He looked like he wanted the ground to swallow him up.

And Mo was muttering to himself, wringing his hands, while his entourage stood dumbly before us. Not four hours into a three-day ordeal and we were coming apart at the seams.

50.

'Enough!' I said, thumping my numb leg. 'The dog could yet turn up or go anywhere. It doesn't matter! Nothing does, except carrying on. Addie's OK. We have a head start. Let's build on it. Mo, lead the way!'

Nobody moved.

'Give me Addie's pack,' I said, reaching for it. 'Here, mine's lighter, tell him to take it,' I said to Mo.

Ignoring my dead leg, I swung Addie's rucksack onto my back. It felt full of bricks, hard edged and heavy. But that was almost reassuring, given the nothingness of my right thigh. I tried to think positively. At least my leg was still capable of keeping me upright. I took a couple of steps and was relieved to see that the signal sent to my foot by my brain got through. Though I couldn't feel much below my right hip, the foot went where I'd hoped it would.

'Come on, Mo!' I forced some brightness into my voice. 'We have to push on. Keep Addie beside you. Set a pace he can follow. And tell everyone to stick close together so we don't get separated. I'll bring up the rear. OK?'

After hesitating for what seemed a dreadful minute but was probably only a few reluctant seconds, Mo nodded. I was so relieved. He addressed the others with more fire in his voice, his hands tightening into fists. A pulse of murmuring agreement went through the group. 'You're right,' he said to me. 'There's no turning back now.'

With that he set off and the others, a string pulled tight behind him, followed one by one. I was last. I'd put myself at the back for two reasons. First, if my limping was obvious, people would be less likely to see it. And second, if I couldn't keep up, I'd slip off the back without harming the rest of the group's chances. Mo was their best hope of making it out of here and I didn't want to be responsible for our failure.

We made slower progress anyway, presumably because of Addie's ankle. The numbness of my leg didn't get to me as much as the uncertainty of the injury. What would happen next? Would the poison – if that's what it was – spread through me, shutting the rest of me down?

My back was slick with sweat. I didn't know if that was a symptom of something worse to come, or just plain fear. I was overheating but the night itself was cooled by the slicing wind.

In a way it was a mercy that I had to concentrate so hard on keeping up without stumbling and falling. Placing my right foot down safely was as tricky as threading a needle in the dark.

I forced myself to keep behind the little lad in his baseball boots, ignore the weight of Addie's pack as best I could, and shut

243

out all my thoughts before they got going. It was impossible to do that entirely: nagging doubts kept sprouting into full-blown pangs of panic as we forged on through the dark.

On we walked, on and on. I was in a complete daze. The numbness of my leg grew into itself, stiffening into a warm, pulsing pain. Was that a good sign or bad? A mile or so further on the pain was sharper still. But I was able to keep up, forcing myself through it.

Amelia was ahead of the kid in the boots. She'd taken hold of the remaining dog's rope. It drifted along beside her as contentedly as it had walked next to me. At one point the scrub we were picking our way through erupted with shrieking birds and the dog barked at them as they blew away. Would the other one have made it back to camp by now? Even if it had, General Sir should still be asleep, surely. We had until morning, and that was hours away.

Except that, astonishingly, as soon as I'd had that thought, the rushing black sky to my left seemed to be turning indigo. Left was east. Within minutes the bruise above the horizon was an umber stripe. We'd walked right through the night and dawn was about to break.

I'd seen the contours of low hills against the night sky, but as it grew lighter the full extent of our exposure became clear: the scrubland was an endless gentle undulation stabbed with the occasional thorny bush or stunted acacia tree. There seemed to be more trees in the distance to our right, but they were a way away.

The pain in my leg had become an occasional hot spasm angling into my hip joint. I rubbed at it as we walked on, the landscape coming into focus. We were tracking a dry stream bed. It formed a rough path of sorts. The dirt, grey-black all night, had an orangey tinge to it in the morning sun. The kid in front's trainers were covered in it. Detail crowded in. Everything was soon pin sharp. As the boy kicked up dust the wind tore it away.

Ahead, Mo stopped. The group concertinaed together as we all caught up. He'd paused us in a culvert. There was a lip of rock running alongside the stream bed here, no more than a metre high. Nevertheless, it was cover of sorts. We'd agreed that we would keep out of sight during the day, but I'd imagined we'd be able to hide away somewhere better than this. Amelia, thinking the same thing, said so.

'The sun is up. Every minute we are in the open is a risk,' said Mo.

'Also, we're exhausted,' Xander agreed.

Amelia looked sceptical.

'We've made progress,' said Mo. 'We're on course to meet the river.'

'I hope it has more water in it than this tributary,' said Amelia doubtfully.

'We could push on just a little further, see if there's somewhere a bit better to lay up,' I suggested. 'Those trees in the distance, for example.'

'They're quite a way.'

As Mo spoke, I spotted something moving over his shoulder. Too fast and smoothly for an animal, a pickup was coming steadily towards us, a great plume of dust shearing into the sky behind it.

'Down!' I shouted. Mo dropped to the ground and everyone else followed suit. We hunched there as the noise of the truck reached us. It was approaching at an angle, and at a constant speed. Since it wasn't picking its way through scrub it had to be travelling along a track of some sort. In all this expanse, how had we wound up next to a road?

We were below the horizon line here but still, the truck was coming in roughly our direction. Were they making a beeline for us? I held my breath. We all did, I'm sure. Nobody moved a muscle as the truck rumbled our way.

51.

I have to admit the thought occurred to me, as we crouched there with bated breath, hoping the truck would pass us by, that the coincidence of us being so close to a track in all that vast emptiness almost seemed too much. I didn't actually think Mo had led us here deliberately, and yet . . .

The engine got louder and louder. It seemed the truck was about to stop right alongside us. But it didn't. I couldn't bring myself to look up, just accepted the blissfully welcome realisation that it wasn't stopping, that instead its engine noise was fading away.

'Thank God for that,' I said under my breath.

'There'd be more point in thanking this ridge of rock,' said Amelia, tapping the embankment with a finger. 'Mo's right. It does in fact shield us from view. Parallax can be helpful.'

'What do we do now, though?' asked Xander.

Mo had unscrewed the lid of a plastic bottle and held it out. 'We wait. We rest, hidden, here. We gather our strength to move again later.'

Xander drank and passed the bottle on to me. The other kids, following Mo's lead, put down the bags and made themselves comfortable. I handed the water bottle along to the little guy with the big trainers. He looked so small sitting in the dirt next to me.

My leg was still pulsing angrily but at least the pain was confined to my thigh now. The bite felt hot. I thought I ought to take a look at it so, using the excuse that I needed the toilet, I leopard-crawled along the gully, tucked myself in behind a boulder, and dropped my trousers.

I gulped at what I saw. I'd definitely been bitten – or stung – by something. A dark puncture dot swam in a pool of purple-yellow, beyond which the skin was an angry red, taut with swelling. No wonder it hurt. Whatever had bitten me couldn't have been that venomous, otherwise I'd be dead, surely? Still, it hurt enough to make me worry the tissue might be damaged or even turn septic. Would I lose my leg?

'No use worrying about that,' I said under my breath. 'And no use scaring the others. Just put up with it, like everything else.'

Talking to myself was daft and reassuring at the same time.

I relieved myself, thinking I might as well while I had the chance. Then I crawled back to the others. Later, I'd check the leg again. For now, I just willed it to feel better. I wasn't the only person in pain. Addie was nursing his ankle, and another of the boys, who I now saw had walked through the night in flip-flops, had injured his left foot, prising the nail up off his big toe. It was encrusted with dirt and dried blood. He wasn't complaining, just inspecting it.

'Tough choice,' said Amelia. 'Obviously he should clean it up to prevent it becoming infected, but if he runs out of water he'll be compromised.'

Ignoring her, Xander knelt next to the boy and dribbled a little from his own bottle onto the wound, motioning for him to dab at it with his shirt sleeve. 'Morale is a thing,' he said to nobody in particular.

Mo passed around some of the congealed slop he'd folded into a bit of plastic. I took a pinch, but I wasn't actually that hungry. The dog eyed what I ate. We'd already given it the last morsel from the traps. I took off its tether: if it wanted to go in search of food, who was I to stop it? But the dog didn't seem to want to leave. Instead it walked round in a circle a couple of times, lay down between me and Mo, and poked its nose under its curled tail.

'We should do the same,' I muttered. 'Rest, as you say.'

Mo agreed. 'One of us should keep watch though.'

I opened my mouth to offer but he'd already turned to one of his troop, a boy with symmetrical raised scar lines down each smooth cheek. With a nod this boy folded his arms across his knees and stayed put as Mo and the others stretched out in the shadow cast by the little escarpment. They did this as if sleeping on the bare earth in the bottom of a gully as the sun rose was entirely normal.

Xander gave a little shrug and followed suit. Instantly he was asleep. He'd kept going uncomplainingly but he was at his limit. Amelia was also spent. She looked gaunt in the harsh light and her hair was matted. But before she curled up on her side like the dog she whispered, 'Your leg, how bad is it?'

'What? It's fine.'

'For me a lie is less reassuring than the truth, always,' she said.

'Something nipped me. It hurt for a bit but it's OK now.'

'If you say so,' she said.

'Get some sleep,' I said.

We both lay back. I covered my eyes with my arm and tried to blot everything out. But I couldn't. I kept thinking about Mum. I had to get back to her, but was I making that more or less likely? We could die out here and nobody would know. Eventually those dark thoughts put me under. But within what felt like seconds – in fact, given the height of the sun, it must have been a couple of hours – something woke me up.

It was the dog growling beside me. I sat up straight and saw that the kid Mo had asked to keep watch was in a crumpled heap, mouth open, asleep. The dog rumble-growled again. That wasn't the only noise, however. Within the rushing wind a tinny, bell-like clinking was coming from behind the outcrop.

I inched my head above it and sure enough I saw a goat nibbling at the scrub about thirty metres away. There was more than one. A herd of them were coming closer. And what was worse, they were accompanied. A lone goatherd trailed along behind them. He looked straight out of the Bible, with a crook, dark robe and headdress, but there was one odd detail in the scene: he was studying his mobile phone as he picked his way towards us.

The dog was still growling. He had also woken Mo, who

clocked the approaching goatherd. The goats would walk on by us if they kept going straight. I put a hand on the back of the dog's neck, intending to soothe it. But dogs aren't daft and the hound was a clever one. He felt the fear my fingertips were transmitting. It was my fault, not his. No doubt he could smell the goats and their owner. I obviously thought they were a threat. So he, the dog, would see them off.

I should have hung on to him but I was too slow.

He leaped out of the gully and his growl burst into full-blooded barking.

52.

The dog's barking didn't scare the goatherd away. Far from it. His goats were rattled by the noise so he raised his head from his phone screen and headed over to investigate. Mo and I ducked down. I hoped in vain that the dog would ease up, but his barking just got louder.

The other kids were waking, confused by the noise, asking questions. Mo hushed them. I hissed an explanation to Xander and Amelia. The dog's bellowing went up another notch. There could only be one reason: the goatherd had to be coming closer.

And he was. He was advancing all the way to the trench. I rummaged in my bag for the empty revolver. If he got as far as poking his head over the lip, I could at least wave the gun at him.

Mo held a finger to his lips. We all stayed stock still. And eventually the dog quietened, leaving just the wind noise laced with goat-bells. I let out a breath, inched my eyes above the embankment, and said, 'What the . . . ?!'

The dog was still right there. But so was the goatherd. He was squatting next to the hound, stroking him. Noticing me, the goatherd stood up. I swear the dog looked at me sheepishly.

The goatherd's face was all creases, his eyes weathered slits. They'd seen everything now. He came towards me, right to the edge of the embankment, and loomed above us all with his hands on his hips.

Mo started talking to the guy but he did not reply, just surveyed us without emotion. Mo tried again, in a different dialect I think, and got exactly the same response. He simply looked us over in turn. As his gaze took me in I realised I was still holding the revolver. He noticed but didn't linger on it particularly. His expression said he came upon bunches of kids – including foreigners armed with ancient handguns – hidden away in the wind-ravaged scrubland most days.

Mo tried talking to the goatherd again, this time handing up a water bottle as he spoke. The guy tilted his head, declining the offer. He seemed to reach a conclusion. Whatever it was, it entailed him simply turning around and walking back to his goats.

We watched him go in silence. The dog looked from him to us and back to him again, and decided tagging along with the goatherd was the better bet. Given how at ease the man was in the environment compared to us, I reckon the dog made a good decision, but I was still sorry to see him go.

'Phew,' said Xander eventually. 'Near miss.'

'What do you mean?' Amelia replied. 'I'd call it a direct hit. He had a very good look at us.'

'Yes, but he didn't seem interested.'

Amelia jerked her thumb Mo's way. He was looking worried. Amelia went on, 'Mo reckons General Sir is known to everyone in these parts. That guy may have looked unbothered but he's probably on the phone to him as we speak.'

It occurred to me, too late, that I could have taken his phone from him. I had a gun, after all. I could have used his phone to call for help. Who I'd have called exactly, other than Mum, I don't know. The thought of speaking to her made my throat knot up. The guy's phone obviously had a signal. How had I let the opportunity go? Should I run after him and make him hand it over?

Xander seemed to read my thoughts. 'We're not muggers,' he said.

'I know, not normally. But we're desperate.'

'If we'd stolen his phone, he'd have wanted revenge,' Xander said. 'He'd definitely have reported us then.'

'Not if we'd tied him up.'

'Making us *worse* than muggers,' Mo said. 'I spun him a story, told him we were out here on patrol.'

'Think he believed you?' asked Xander.

Mo looked away.

'Thought not,' I said.

Xander said, 'He's bound to tell someone he's seen us.'

'Making the only logical plan obvious,' said Amelia with a sigh.

I could see where she was going. 'We can't make him un-see us, but we can make *where* he saw us history.'

254

'Yes,' said Mo. 'We can't stay here any longer.'

Beside me, Xander's shoulders sank. As brightly as I could I said, 'We've had a bit of rest. The sooner we get to safety, the better. Agreed?'

Xander nodded, but I knew he was exhausted. Setting off again so soon was the last thing he wanted to do. I felt the same way. Now that the adrenaline sparked by the goatherd's visit had evaporated, I felt giddy with tiredness. Also, my leg was pulsing with heat again. I didn't want to look at it, much less walk on it, but I had to. Like the other boys in the trench we gathered up our things at Mo's instruction.

The goatherd had been heading north. We set off to the south-west, following the dried-up stream bed again, at a tangent to the dirt road. I brought up the rear, and I don't mind admitting it was a struggle. The wind had swung round so that we were heading straight into it, and if anything it had intensified.

Combined with the heaviness of my leg, it felt like I was wading through treacle to keep up. The giddiness got worse too. I began to worry it was something more than tiredness, and I couldn't shift the thought of poison running through my veins. We'd been going for about an hour and the sun, a white blur behind the clouds, was high in the sky, but the cloud layer was thick and black, so the landscape was bathed in a weird flat light. Everything looked as dead as I felt inside.

The wind grew more hellish still. It buzzed with heavy static, full of grit scoured from the great emptiness ahead. I kept my face lowered and my eyes half shut, squinting at Amelia's heels ahead of me, forcing myself to keep up, because keeping up was all I could do to get back to Mum. Mum, Mum, Mum. The word was a drumbeat in my head. Without it I could not have carried on.

Mum.

Mum.

Mum.

Out of nowhere an almighty thunderbolt blew the whole world a brilliant, deafening white. It was louder and brighter than any lightning strike I'd ever witnessed, and it stopped us dead. We all cowered. The lightning bolt had struck the ground just behind us. The air smelled of burnt earth.

I turned, expecting to see a scorch mark or leaping flames, but in the immediate aftermath of the thunderbolt the gloom had thickened again. Despite this, I saw the men in the distance. This was no random car or wandering goatherd. It was six armed men, rifles slung across their midriffs, purposefully headed our way.

53.

The men were two hundred metres behind us, two-fifty at most. We'd never outrun them. Or at least, not all of us would. I was reeling from the lightning blast, pulsing with poison, delirious with exhaustion, but I still saw the situation for what it was. The men were coming for us all, but we weren't all of equal value to them. Xander, Amelia and I could be ransomed; the others were cannon fodder. And let's face it, in my state I was the slowest across this terrain. I grabbed hold of Mo and shouted, 'Run for it! You and the rest. The three of us will hold them here.'

'What?!'

'They're less likely to hurt us.'

'You think?'

'We're just money to them. For ransom, not war. You guys might still get away. Go!'

Mo stepped closer, put both hands on my shoulders and looked me straight in the face. 'I'm not leaving you here,' he said simply.

'Go!' I repeated. 'We're wasting time . . .'

But none of the other kids had moved off. They were all still rooted to the spot, watching the men approach. I knew it was hopeless, but I couldn't do the same. I grabbed hold of Mo with one hand and Amelia with the other and staggered forward into the howling gale. They came with me, and Xander followed too, and a few of the other kids trailed in our wake, but I was limping so badly I couldn't even run properly.

There was a metallic *pop* and the rushing wind split above us. Another shot followed, fizzing overhead. On I limped. But I was dragging the others now.

'Jack,' said Xander. 'It's OK, Jack, we tried.'

The next shot hit the ground to our right, sending rock chippings and dust into the air.

'We can't outrun bullets,' Xander said, gently pulling me to a stop.

'Or indeed them,' said Amelia, who'd turned to face the advancing men.

I turned too. They'd halved the distance between us and they weren't even running at speed, just jogging steadily towards us. As they came closer our little group gathered together. I looked from child to child. All of them had their eyes on the ground. They were so utterly resigned to whatever was coming next, I could have wept. The escape plan, such as it was, had failed, and since it had been my plan it was my fault.

I lifted my gaze to meet the approaching men. Now that we'd stopped, they had slowed to a walk. They were close enough for me to see them properly. I expected to find General Sir among the six, possibly with Kayd and Liban. They would want revenge. So be it. It took me a second to realise that none of the three were there.

'Uniforms,' Xander murmured.

'I was thinking the same thing,' said Amelia.

In my befuddled state I was slow to catch on, but yes, I recognised the uniform too. These guys were Somali military, dressed like the men who'd visited General Sir's compound. In fact, the nearest man *was* the heavyset soldier who'd accompanied the Leopard guy to buy recruits. He had big sweat patches under his arms and a sheen across his forehead.

But he wasn't the reason my skin was crawling. That was the fault of the last man who came into view as the soldiers fanned out. Also wearing desert fatigues, but not the same government issue, this man was unarmed, white and unmistakable: Mr Leopold – the Leopard – whose photograph I'd first seen on Mum's laptop screen. Unlike the big soldier, he wasn't puffing. He looked us over with a hint of amusement in his deadpan grey eyes.

'Jack, Amelia, Xander: great to catch up with you,' he said at length. 'And on such a lovely day. Quite a lightning strike, eh?'

He didn't wait for a response. Instead he turned to the assembled soldiers and conversed with them in their own language.

'What's going on?' Amelia asked Mo.

'They're working out who takes who.'

'What do you mean?' I asked.

'The Leopard guy wants to split us up,' he muttered. 'He's going to take you three on. We're being dealt with separately.'

The negotiation, if that's what it was, seemed not to be going entirely smoothly. There were raised voices. A tall soldier with neatly rolled shirtsleeves appeared to object to what the Leopard was proposing. He was chewing something red and spat it out at the Leopard's feet, both hands cradling his gun across his chest.

'This doesn't feel good,' Amelia said beside me.

I knew what she meant, but something about the Leopard's calm was reassuring: he seemed more bored than upset about the tall soldier's objection. He held himself very still and upright, as if to say the situation was simple as he saw it.

By contrast, a million thoughts were piling through my head. How had they tracked us down so easily? Was it a tip-off from the goatherd, or had we been seen from the road, or was our route that predictable?

If they were splitting us up that had to mean the Leopard had decided to claim the ransom money after all. We were in his hands now. Although I hated him for it, I had a reluctant sense this was probably a good thing. But what would happen to Mo and the others? What did 'dealt with' mean?

'The rings,' I said to Amelia.

'What about them?'

'Quick, give them to me.'

'OK.' She knelt, yanked open the neck of her left shoe, rolled down her sock, and pulled out a little roll of material which she'd wedged next to her ankle. With one eye on the negotiating adults, I unfolded it surreptitiously. Even in this dull light the rings glowed. I quickly balled the little parcel up again and turned to Mo.

'Take these,' I said.

'Eh?'

'Just take them. They're more use to you than us. Help this lot with them,' I said, taking in the abject kids around us. 'Wait for the right moment, with the right guard, then buy their freedom.'

'I can't accept,' said Mo, pushing the rings back at me. 'They are your currency.'

'Worth more to you,' I said. 'Please.'

Amelia said, 'He's right, Mo. It makes intrinsic sense and you know it.'

What she meant by 'intrinsic' I had no idea, but Mo nodded.

'Just hide them before . . .' Xander petered out as the adults swung their attention back to us. Mercifully Mo had already accepted the little package. He slid it behind his back.

The soldiers were in among us now, pushing and shoving, separating Xander, Amelia and me from the group. The Leopard stood to one side. He had his phone out and was tapping at it. Meanwhile his fat accomplice loomed over the three of us, one hand on the stock of his rifle, everything about him ordering 'stay put'.

The tall guy with the rolled sleeves seemed to be in charge of the other government soldiers. He barked at Mo and his rag-tag group, prompting them to jostle into two lines. Mo was in the middle of the nearest one. I've never known a tougher, cleverer or more resourceful kid, but right then he looked small and weary and utterly beaten.

The tall guy with the rolled sleeves spat out another gout of red gunk and gave a further order, at which the phalanx of recaptured children started back the way we'd come. Mo turned briefly to the three of us as they were marched away. He tried to smile but his face was filled with despair.

54.

The fat, sweat-stained soldier used his gun barrel to point the way he wanted us to go. I hobbled along with the others in front of him. The Leopard followed last. My limping was pretty obvious. Still, he felt the need to point it out.

'You've been in the wars, Jack.'

I said nothing.

'Is it painful?'

I wasn't about to give him the satisfaction of a truthful answer, so opted for more silence instead.

'Well, we don't have far to go. I'm sure you can make it.'

He actually sounded quite concerned but was probably just worried he'd get less of a ransom for damaged goods. I gritted my teeth against the pain and kept going. I was feeling more and more light-headed. The relentless wind kept up its scouring. In my addled state it sounded like the sea, a jet, a chainsaw.

I couldn't bear the thought of what might happen to Mo and the others, but it seemed to be all I could think about as we staggered on. He'd been right about the impossibility of escape. However General Sir punished them would be on me. I'd forced Mo to flee the camp, co-opted a band of innocent youngsters to come with us, and led the lot of them straight into a deeper danger than they already faced. I'd failed Xander and Amelia. I'd failed myself. But worst of all, somehow, I'd failed Mo and his helpers.

At some point my pace slowed so much Xander decided I needed helping. He dragged my right arm around his shoulders and took some of my weight. His shoulders were bony. Next, Amelia had hold of me from the other side. The three of us staggered on into the gale. It sounded like an engine now. In fact, it *was* an engine. A jeep was tearing up dust as it raced our way.

'We should. Flag it. Need to. Down,' I muttered. I could tell I wasn't making much sense, but the jeep – which turned into a Land Rover as it got closer – seemed our last hope. If we could just alert the driver, maybe he'd save us. 'Wave. Help,' I managed, but nobody did anything about it.

Miraculously, not fifty metres away, the Land Rover slowed to a halt. We were headed straight towards it. Maybe its driver would in fact come to the rescue. A ridiculous hope, I know, but it took me an age to realise the obvious: the 4x4 was coming for us deliberately because the Leopard had called for it.

The very same soldier who'd accompanied him and his fat friend to buy boys for the army from General Sir was behind the wheel. We had marched back to the dirt road. Now the Leopard himself was opening up the Land Rover's rear door and, since I seemed to be too weak to climb up onto the running board, helping Xander and Amelia bundle me inside.

The adults took the front seats and once everyone was aboard the doors shut with a *clump-clump*. This cut the wind dead. In the silence before the 4x4 took off Amelia whispered two words: 'Poor Mo.'

A wave of guilt swept through me so hard I groaned out loud.

Xander patted my shoulder and muttered, 'They have something to bargain with at least.'

'Correct,' said Amelia. 'Taking the rings into consideration, they're better off than they were beforehand.'

Xander was doing his best to be positive but his, 'So are we, right?' sounded tentative.

The Leopard was just there, right in front of us. He craned round in his seat to look us over, even managing to fake some concern with those steady, wide-spaced eyes. I wanted to ask him where he was taking us, what would happen to Mo now, and how he could live with himself buying children and sending them off to war. But I couldn't. I barely had enough energy to sit upright, much less speak. I slumped sideways across Xander and more or less lost consciousness. I could still hear people talking but they were making less sense than the jolting of the SUV on the rough road. Before I passed out entirely, I heard just one word, repeated by the Leopard. 'Exhaustion.'

55.

Next thing I knew, I was lying in bed staring at a strip light. It was buzzing, restful as a lazy honeybee on a summer afternoon. And someone was gently kneading the bones in my left hand. I turned to thank whoever it was and saw Mum.

Mum.

Mum?

'Mum!'

I tried to hug her but something – a drip stuck in my right arm, it turned out – held me back. Mum leaned over me anyway, tears filling her eyes.

'Amelia? Xander?' My voice was papery.

'They're OK, Jack, don't worry. You're all going to be fine.'

'My leg.'

I couldn't feel it, which worried me for a second, but my knee jerked up towards me when I told it to, so it was still there.

'Yes, the doctor spotted that. He's given you antibiotics

to kill the infection and pain medication. The drip's just saline. You were all very dehydrated. What stung you?'

'I don't know.'

'It doesn't matter now. You're in safe hands here.'

'Where are we?'

'Nairobi. You arrived late yesterday night.'

'I'm sorry.'

'Sorry?'

'This was all my fault.'

'Nonsense! Pete explained everything.'

'But I insisted on the extra dive and I made us fall for the pirates' fake . . . wait, Pete!'

'Yes, Pete. He was in the water for six hours, but he knew which way to swim and he made it ashore, a feat he's justifiably proud of.'

Tears were rolling down my cheeks now. Mum brushed them away with her fingertips. I stared up at her. To be together again, to feel her fingers on my face, was incredible. And Pete had made it to safety. The relief I felt about that, combined with the ferocity of my love for Mum in that moment, knocked the words out of me. I simply couldn't speak. It didn't matter. We sat together in silence for a while, letting everything sink in.

Eventually Mum said, 'You're safe now. Listen, I promised I'd tell Amelia and Xander when you woke up . . .'

She wasn't gone long and she had no luck persuading Amelia to wait before coming to see me until I'd slept some more. Amelia simply barged into my room with an, 'If he's finally awake, he's awake.'

Xander was close behind her, saying, 'That's a pretty obvious statement for you in particular to make.'

I'd pushed myself up into a sitting position. Washed and wearing clean clothes, both my friends looked newly minted in the bright hospital light. I'd grown used to them in General Sir's hand-me-down rags. The funny thing was, dressed in their own stuff, it was now obvious how much they'd shrunk. Xander's T-shirt looked like it was hung on a hanger. And Amelia's cheekbones were knife-blades.

'You gave us a bit of a scare back there, Jack,' said Xander.

'But that's beside the point now,' said Amelia. 'My real beef is with why you didn't tell us you'd been envenomated.'

'By which you mean bitten,' Xander said, 'or stung.'

I shrugged. 'You couldn't have done anything to help, so what was the point?'

She gave a 'humph' but didn't elaborate.

I turned back to Mum. 'The ransom,' I said. 'We really didn't want you to have to pay it.'

'I know,' she said. 'I got the message.'

'So, I'm sorry about that too,' I said.

'You needn't be.'

'Well, I am.'

Xander cut in. 'No, she means you actually don't need to worry about the ransom.'

'Nobody does,' Mum added. But I could tell she was just trying to be kind to me, and I couldn't stop myself shaking my head.

Amelia spelled it out: 'Because nobody paid a ransom, Jack.'

I sighed and shut my eyes: for Amelia to feel the need to lie to me she must have thought I was in an awful state.

'You did brilliantly just to survive,' Mum was saying. 'The pirates, the camp; to make a run for it like that took guts. And it helped. With no armed resistance it made your rescue easier.'

I pushed myself up in the bed again. 'Rescue?'

'Even if I hadn't got your "no ransom" message I'd have done everything I could to avoid paying one. It's a matter of principle. As soon as Pete confirmed what had happened, I swung into action.'

Xander said, 'Your mum sent that Leopard guy to get us out of there. Isn't that right, Mrs Courtney?'

'It is,' she said. 'We were going to try and extract you from the camp itself, once we tracked you down to it, but obviously that would have been much riskier. You made the job a lot easier by breaking out.'

What she was saying made little sense to me. I searched her face for an explanation. Was she lying, hoping to make me feel less guilty? That's not Mum's style, not her style at all. And yet. I realised I'd been holding my breath, and now let it out, literally deflating in front of her.

'If you kids could give Jack and me a minute, I'd appreciate it,' she said.

'As in sixty seconds?' said Amelia, only half joking.

'Come on,' said Xander, leading her out. 'See you in a bit.'

'Nobody paid a ransom,' Mum repeated when they'd left. 'I respected your wishes.'

'Well, even if that's true you still had to pay a damn mercenary,' I muttered.

269

'Jonny is no mercenary, Jack.'

'Who's Jonny? I'm talking about the Leopard.'

'Leopard, Leopold, those are aliases. His name is Jonny Armfield. And he's one of the good guys.'

The world was still a bit fuzzy, but I knew one thing for sure. 'Actually,' I muttered, 'you're dead wrong about that.'

'He found you, didn't he?'

'Yeah, yeah. I'm grateful and everything. But that's his specialty. Finding kids for money. Though mostly he sells them off as soldiers.'

'No,' said Mum.

'I've seen him do it! He came to the camp and took a load away. And just yesterday he consigned my good friend Mo, together with all the rest of the kids who tried to escape with us, back to that hellhole. What do you think will happen to them now he's done that?!'

'Jack, you were my concern. You and Amelia and Xander.'

Even as she insisted this, I knew she was thinking of the kids she'd not been able to help, and was wishing she'd been able to do more, so I let up. 'Thanks for paying him to rescue us at least,' I said.

'I didn't pay him.'

Now she was making no sense at all. 'Mercenaries do stuff – bad stuff – for *money*. They're not charities, Mum. Don't expect me to believe he did it for free.'

'Not for free, no. But for something more significant than money.'

An electric pulse went through me as she said that. It connected the dots, just for a second, and I did not like the shape they made one bit. Mum, seeing the pained realisation in my face, started talking quickly, wanting to head it off no doubt, but in fact making everything worse.

'Jonny and I go way back. He was in the army when we first met, Special Forces, and now he's in Intelligence. He was out here working. In fact, he's the real reason we came to Zanzibar. I wanted you to meet him. Not in the way you did, of course. We were trying to organise a simple face-to-face on neutral ground when you were abducted.'

'The guy buys and sells child soldiers,' I said. 'Why would I want to meet somebody like that?'

'It may have seemed that way, but trust me, he does the exact opposite. And I wanted you to meet him because of who he is. You asked the question. He is the answer.'

I knew what she was going to say – that this Jonny guy was my actual father – but I managed to blot it out somehow, and here's what I was thinking: Mum had been conned by a bad man before. No matter what she said now, she was wrong to think Jonny, Leopold, whoever, was a good person. I'd seen him be the opposite of good. I said nothing, just sat there as she went on.

'But listen. Why don't you let him explain what he actually does in person? He wants to talk to you. Now that you're out of that hellhole, as you put it, he can drop the cover persona and be himself. Not today, but soon, when you've got more of your strength back, talk to him. Let me arrange that.'

I'd seen the guy hand over money for child recruits; I'd watched him condemn Mo and his friends to near certain death. Now, as I lay back against the cool hospital pillow and shut my eyes, I saw the hopeless fear etched on poor Mo's face as he was led away. With my eyes still closed I answered Mum in a whisper. 'I'm pleased we're safe. I'm sorry I put us in danger in the first place. Thank you for getting us out, for organising a rescue. I'm grateful for that guy's help. But whoever he is he's not my father and no, I don't want to meet him today, tomorrow, or next week. In fact, I never want to see his face again for as long as I live.'

Epilogue

A few months later, after what passed for a return to normality – or the drudgery of school, at least – Xander, Amelia and I met up during the autumn half term to go mountain biking. It was a crisp day with a bright blue sky full of contrails. The bracken had already turned brown but most of the trees still had their leaves. We were close to where I live in the Surrey Hills, about to drop into Captain Clunk, one of my favourite trails, and Xander had paused to let some air out of his front tyre. He'd pumped it up too hard that morning before we started. Or at least that was his excuse for washing out in a flat corner on the last run.

Amelia was looking at her phone. I checked mine too and discovered I had a voicemail from a number I didn't recognise. I reckoned it was probably spam, but Xander was still fiddling with his tyre so I pressed play and held the phone to my ear.

'Hey,' said an instantly familiar voice. 'It's me, Mo.'

'No way!' I shouted, hitting pause.

'No way what?' asked Amelia. 'We're going to need some context.'

Xander had stood up from his bike and was looking at me closely. I put the phone on speaker and started the message again. Even the birds seemed to quieten down as it played.

'Hey, it's me, Mo. I hope you guys are safely home. I thought you might want to know I made it out too, thanks to you. A few of us did. Your treasure worked. Remember that very tall guard the Leopard turned us over to? Well, he saw the sense in trading: a boy for a ring was his best offer. For all seven pieces he'd let seven of us run for it, while he took the rest back to General Sir. We made it to the river and across the border eventually; it wasn't actually that far but our pace was very slow. In Kenya we split up. Long story short, I reached the capital and found work as a fixer for a travel agent. It doesn't pay much but I'm allowed to sleep in the storeroom behind the shop and the owner's wife makes great fried chicken. So, I have a roof over my head and enough to eat and that's a start. Without those rings I wouldn't have stood a chance. Thanks again. Who knows what's coming next? When I find out I'll let you know!'

The three of us looked at one another. I bit my lip, a lump in my throat. To buy time for it to pass I played the message again, but Mo's voice – it was definitely him – sounding so cheerful made the lump bigger, not smaller. Luckily Amelia cut in with, 'I always thought someone as resourceful as Mo would find a way out sooner or later. The rings just expedited his self-extraction, in my opinion.'

'You mean sped up his escape,' said Xander.

'That's what the words mean, yes,' said Amelia.

They were jousting but smiling at one another. We'd all been gutted after the Leopard split us up from Mo and the others. To hear that some of them at least, and Mo in particular, had made it to safety, was the best news possible. When Xander finally sorted his bike, I rode that trail flat out with the biggest grin on my face.

I couldn't wait to tell Mum, so I headed straight home after that. She was in the study poring over maps of the Arctic tundra. Apparently a consortium of oil companies was planning on digging up a load of pristine wilderness to get at the gas beneath it, and Mum's latest thing was coordinating efforts to stop them.

Since we got back from Kenya, I'd filled her in on the full story with Mo, and I knew she'd been feeling guilty that the Leopard hung him and the others out to dry, so I hoped this news would mean a lot to her too.

It did. She beamed at me and said, 'I knew all that treasure-hunting was for a purpose.'

'Originally I was going to put what we found towards your coral conservation project,' I said.

'I know, and I'd have been so grateful. But this makes more sense given what happened.'

And that would have been that. Mum had known better than to bring up the Leopard – or Jonny, if that's what he was really called – since our return, and although she could now say his actions hadn't cost Mo his life after all, she didn't.

I left her to her work and went down to the kitchen to fix myself some lunch. While I was stuffing a bagel full of pickle, ham, cheese and mayonnaise the doorbell rang. It was just the postman; he'd rung because he needed a signature for a recorded delivery. I did the honours, thanked him, and went back inside.

It turned out the padded envelope I'd signed for was addressed to me. I hadn't ordered anything online and wasn't expecting a delivery of any sort. With the bagel clamped between my teeth I ripped open the envelope, mildly curious to see what was inside. When the contents spilled out I opened my mouth in surprise, dropping the bagel in among the seven gold rings rolling around on the countertop.

What the . . . ?

I checked the envelope and fished out a note. It was handwritten in black ink on a square of thick cream paper.

Dear J, I understand your reluctance to meet with me. Nevertheless, I hope that by returning these rings, which I have retrieved on your behalf, I can prove that all was not as it seemed in Somalia. My actions, which you witnessed there, were part of an ongoing operation. Had I revealed my true identity I would have jeopardised that operation's goal, which included shutting down camps such as General Sir's permanently. I hope you'll give me the opportunity to explain myself in person one day. For now, you should know your friend Mo is safe. Though I was unable to liberate him and the others when I caught up with you, for fear of blowing my own cover, I assure you that

*freeing all the children in the camp was always
my intention. With these rings you – and he – beat
me to it. They served their purpose. I have great
pleasure in returning them to their rightful owner.
Yours, J.*

The rings were unmistakably the ones we'd found with our detectors. The little earring was even among them. Amelia had smuggled the lot through our ordeal, and I had last seen them as I pressed them into Mo's hand. How had this man hunted them down? I had no idea, yet here they were, indisputably, on the kitchen work surface.

I gathered them up. In a minute I'd show them to Mum. Maybe they'd help fund her new tundra preservation initiative. She'd offered to take me up there – somewhere cold for a change! – to look at what was at stake. This would be a way of showing a bit of enthusiasm for the cause.

I'd talk to her about all that in a bit, just as soon as I'd finished my lunch. I read the note over and over as I ate that bagel. Like all the food I'd eaten since our return, it tasted magnificent. I smiled when I finished it.

The note was written in solid, regular handwriting.

Dear J, it began. And *Yours, J*, it ended.

Despite myself, I liked that.

*Look out for the next Jack Courtney Adventure,
SHOCKWAVE, out now!*

Wilbur Smith is an international bestselling author, having sold over 130 million copies of his incredible adventure novels. His Courtney family saga is the longest running series in publishing history, and with the Jack Courtney Adventures he brings the series to a new generation.

Chris Wakling read his first Wilbur Smith book when he was Jack's age: fourteen. He writes novels and travel journalism, and is available for events and interviews.

For all the latest information about Wilbur, visit:
www.wilbursmithbooks.com
facebook.com/WilburSmith
www.wilbur-niso-smithfoundation.org

Wilbur Smith donates twenty per cent of profits received from the sale of this copy to The Wilbur & Niso Smith Foundation. The Foundation's focus is to encourage adventure writing and literacy and find new talent.

For more information, please visit
www.wilbur-niso-smithfoundation.org

THE WILBUR & NISO SMITH
FOUNDATION

Piccadilly
P R E S S

Thank you for choosing a Piccadilly Press book.

If you would like to know more about our authors, our books or if you'd just like to know what we're up to, you can find us online.

www.piccadillypress.co.uk

And you can also find us on:

We hope to see you soon!